Praise for

The Details

"This beautiful, mov[...]lone portraits that, together[...]re of the portraitist. The nar[...]separate memoir from fiction, [...] present, and self from other, which evokes the spell of fever during which it was written. The miraculous sort of novel that fuses with our personal memories and becomes part of us."

—Hernan Diaz, Pulitzer Prize–winning and
New York Times bestselling author of *Trust*

"*The Details* is about relationships, about love, about parents and children . . . about all of it. The little observations about being young, and about growing up, and about getting lost by accident, and getting lost on purpose, searching for yourself in everyone else . . . damn it, I've underlined half of the book. I wish I could write like this."

—Fredrik Backman,
#1 *New York Times* bestselling author

"The literal fever that begins the book mirrors the feverish beginnings and endings of these relationships, as well as the fever of reading—how it forces the reader inward, then leaves an invisible imprint in its wake. Genberg's marvelous prose is also a kind of fever, mesmerizing and hot to the touch."

—*New York Times Book Review*

"In four succinct and arresting portraits, the narrator of *The Details* remembers the people who have shaped her life. At once humorous and heartbreaking, this book is an ode to the different kinds of love that form us. It asks how we hold on to the people who touch us, how we remember them, and whether we should ever let them go. I won't forget this beautiful book."

—Jenna Clake, author of *Disturbance*

"A fever dream . . . Genberg's prose is a feat of characterization, a triumph of lending language and profundity to observations of daily life. . . . I didn't read it so much as subconsciously absorb it."

—Literary Hub

"Takes the reader on a woozy, affecting dive into desire, domination, and memory. . . . *The Details* was a bestseller in Sweden, where it won the August Prize for best fiction book of 2022. An elegant translation by Kira Josefsson deserves to repeat that success. [Genberg has an] empathetic approach to the quirks and failings of her characters. All there is to the self, observes the narrator, are the 'traces of the people we rub up against.' The greatest achievement of this short and affecting novel is its presentation of those encounters as one long fever dream."

—*Financial Times*

"Emotionally nuanced and formally innovative, Ia Genberg's beautiful novel *The Details* manages the remarkable feat of painting a whole picture of a single life, solely via the lives of the people who have touched it. This is a novel that, through its very bones, encapsulates one of the most important ideas of our current political moment—the necessity of connection, and our vulnerability to one other."

—Susannah Dickey, author of *Tennis Lessons*

"The non-linear narrative renders the protagonist both vivid and obscure—the perfect conduit for this compelling, uncannily precise meditation on transience."

—*The Observer* (London)

The Details

The Details

A Novel

Ia Genberg

Translated by Kira Josefsson

HarperVia

An Imprint of HarperCollins*Publishers*

THE DETAILS. Copyright © 2022 by Ia Genberg. English translation copyright © 2023 by Kira Josefsson. All rights reserved. Printed in the United States of America. No part of this book may be used or reproduced in any manner whatsoever without written permission except in the case of brief quotations embodied in critical articles and reviews. For information, address HarperCollins Publishers, 195 Broadway, New York, NY 10007.

HarperCollins books may be purchased for educational, business, or sales promotional use. For information, please email the Special Markets Department at SPsales@harpercollins.com.

Originally published as *Detaljerna* in Sweden in 2022 by Weyler Förlag.

FIRST HARPERCOLLINS PAPERBACK PUBLISHED IN 2024

Designed by Janet Evans-Scanlon

Library of Congress Cataloging-in-Publication Data is available upon request.

ISBN 978-0-06-330972-2

24 25 26 27 28 LBC 5 4 3 2 1

Johanna

After a few days of the virus in my body I come down with a fever, which is followed by an urge to return to a particular novel. It's only once I sit down in bed and open the book that I understand why. There's an inscription on the title page, made in blue ballpoint and inimitable handwriting:

May 29, 1996

Get well soon.

There are crêpes and cider at Fyra Knop.

I'm waiting until we can go there again.

Kisses (they would prefer to be on your lips),

Johanna

It was malaria back then; I'd been infected a couple of weeks prior by an East African mosquito in a tent outside of the Serengeti and fell sick once we were home again. I was admitted to Hudiksvall Hospital and nobody could understand why all my results were off the charts; when at last they gave me the diagnosis, the doctors lined up to get a look at the woman with the exotic affliction. A fire blazed behind my brow, and I woke at dawn every morning at the hospital from the sound of my own breathing and a headache unlike anything I'd ever experienced before. Following our trip to Tanzania, I'd gone straight to Hälsingland to visit my grandfather on his deathbed. Instead I fell ill and nearly died myself. I spent more than a week at the hospital, but by the time Johanna gave me this novel, I was curled up in our bedroom in Hägersten, where they had taken me by ambulance via a liver biopsy in Uppsala. I don't remember the results—there's not much I can recall from that summer—but I'll never forget our apartment, the book, or her. The novel disappeared inside the fever and headache, fused with them, and somewhere in that mix is the line that runs all the way to today, a vein of emotion electrified by illness and fear, which is what propels me to the bookcase on this afternoon to find that specific novel. Ruthless fever and headache, fretful thoughts crowding behind the eyes, the whooshing of impending distress: I recognize it all because I've experienced it before—the boxes of useless painkillers on the floor by the bed, the bottles of sparkling water I guzzle without any reprieve to my thirst. The images start rolling the instant I shut my eyes: horses' hooves in a dry desert, dank basements full of mute ghosts, big vowels screaming at me—it's the full standard menu of nightmares I've had since I was a small child, only with the added sprinkling of death and annihilation that is the territory of illness.

Literature was our favorite game. Johanna and I introduced each other to authors and themes, to eras and regions and singular works, to older books and contemporary books and books of different genres. We had similar tastes but opinions divergent enough to make our discussions interesting. There were certain things we didn't agree on (Oates, Bukowski), others that left us both unmoved (Gordimer, fantasy), and some we both loved (Klas Östergren, Eyvind Johnson's Krilon trilogy, Lessing). I could tell how she felt about a book based on how fast she worked her way through it. If she was reading fast (Kundera, all crime fiction), I knew she was bored and rushing to be done, and if she was going too slow (*The Tin Drum*, all sci-fi), she was equally bored but had to struggle to reach the last page.

She thought it was her duty to finish a book she'd started—just as she finished all her courses, papers, and projects. There was a deep-rooted sense of obedience in her, a kind of deference to the task at hand no matter how hopeless it might seem. She must have gotten that from her parents, from their creativity and unflappable dedication. In her view this commitment to completion allowed her to enter the future unencumbered, a way of maintaining what she called "a clean slate." Life, in Johanna's world, was lived in one direction, and that direction was forward, only forward. It's how we differed from each other: I rarely completed anything big. After a year of temping in various Pressbyrån convenience stores, I enrolled in multiple university courses, all of which I would end up either dropping or deferring to the future, until I started to write more seriously. And not even at that point, when I'd resolved to dedicate myself full-time to becoming an author, did I manage to follow the path I'd laid out for myself. Instead I spent my days strolling around Aspudden, Mälarhöjden, Midsommarkransen, Axelsberg. In this era the neighborhoods on the city's outskirts still had a certain seediness to them, with motorcycle clubs and tattoo studios and dim video rental stores with tanning beds. The subway stations were dank and dirty. All manner of people lived side by side, white-collar workers who went to work with briefcases in hand, artists who rented cheap studios in the industrial areas, junkies whose drug dens were regularly raided by the cops, old men with leathery skin who spent all day drinking in the town squares; these people all lived alongside one another in the three-story buildings that lined the winding main streets. These buildings housed cramped storefronts that sold foreign spices and simple restaurants with brown interiors where I'd sit in a corner, an empty plate on a plastic tray in front of me as I finished the dregs of my light beer while watching the other early afternoon patrons. There'd be a notebook in front of me, paired with a carefully selected pen, but I rarely made use of these implements. I might have given the impression of being dedicated but I was not, and the book stack on my nightstand always included one or two titles I'd abandoned midway through. I preferred books with a pull so strong I couldn't get out. It was the same way with most things in life and as a result my responsibilities were few, perhaps too few. In fact I'd rarely encountered a responsibility I didn't reject. This general principle didn't make for any "clean slates," and I assume that Johanna could only view my inherent inertia as a challenge. There was something about her speed and enthusiasm that gave me a bit of velocity, made things happen. Maybe this characteristic was what made me feel so safe in our relationship: she had started on me and wouldn't give up. She wasn't going anywhere; she'd never yield to an impulse to leave. I relaxed and surrendered. She was so thorough, so affectionate and loyal. Would breaking up ever occur to someone like her? No, I thought. No, never.

The book in my hand is *The New York Trilogy*. Auster: hermetic but nimble, both simple and twisted, at once paranoid and crystalline, and with an open sky between every word. On that point we agreed, Johanna and I, and a couple of weeks later, when the fever subsided, I read it again, now looking for flaws. I wanted to find out if the series was in fact obvious or boring but not a single thing was off about it, and soon thereafter I read *Moon Palace* and was again spellbound. Auster turned into a true north of mine when it came to both reading and writing, even after I forgot about him and stopped reading his new books as they came out. His discerning simplicity became an ideal, initially associated with his name though it endured on its own. Some books stay in your bones long after their titles and details have slipped from memory. When I finally went to Brooklyn for the first time, I looked up his address as if it was the most natural thing to do. It was a couple of years into the new millennium, and Johanna had long since left me for someone else, a sudden and brutal departure, stone-cold. By the time I was staring at the stoop of the brownstone where Paul Auster and Siri Hustvedt lived their lives and wrote their books, I was in a serious relationship with a man who in that moment was eating pancakes with my daughter at a nearby café. The multiple folded properties of time made it so that I could hear Johanna say something about chance, something I wouldn't understand until much later, made it so that we both could think that we saw something moving behind the curtains on the top floor.

Like my current fever, that malaria infection installed a sense of eternity in my body; the illness felt like a permanent state. We had traveled to visit two friends of hers who were working in "the humanitarian aid world," a world that seemed highly capacious. After two weeks of hanging out with them, I still didn't understand what their jobs were. One of them was making a movie for some organization, and this movie was potentially going to screen at a conference, if the conference did indeed happen and if the movie did end up being made; whereas the other friend didn't seem to do much more than tag along while carrying camera tripods. They were going to spend three months there before heading down south, and that night in the tent outside the Serengeti was our last night in the country. Nobody noticed the mosquito that bit me even though we shared a mosquito net, but on the plane home I found three itchy bumps on my elbow. Johanna had nothing. Technically the fever didn't last more than two or three weeks, four at most, but it felt like I was bedridden for months. Johanna dabbed my forehead and brought me pastries from the bakery on the square, bite-size to fit my tiny appetite. She said she worried about my jutting hipbones though I could tell she was secretly fascinated by them. She made soups with cream and fed me bread she toasted in the oven with big pats of butter that sank into the crumb. I was grateful for all of it, for the food and the gifts, the paperbacks she inscribed with poetic flair. She hailed from an affectionate upper-middle-class family in Täby and this was how they gave presents: at random occasions and in elegant wrapping with beautiful cards slipped under the bows. There was a festive aspect to receiving one of these gifts, even when it was a simple offering slid across the table at lunch. In her world it wasn't just about content and packaging, but also about the degree of surprise, about timing and allusions to the past and a potential future. Every gift was part of a web of references, winks, and tacit information. With time the accrual of these presents became a burden; I would never be able to catch up. Her gifts were too many, too expensive, and too full of promises. Moreover, she had an eye for beauty that I lacked; she could find the perfect watch in a museum store; she bought a tray with a print of a film poster, *Summer with Monika*, at a movie theater threatened with closure. I still have both. My kids have asked me about this Monika, who she was and with whom she had that black-and-white summer, and the now-defunct watch is stuffed into a toiletry bag without its wristband, but I've never come across one as nice. Because of her brutal departure I tossed some of her presents and stowed others in an attic workshop, with the intention of bringing them back out again as my feelings cooled. It was never about financial value; money wasn't something we talked about. She didn't take out a student loan like the rest of us (we initially met in a journalism class at the university); instead she had a Visa card linked to a bank account that was regularly replenished by her parents. For me, who moved out and started supporting myself at age sixteen, and who'd dropped out of college several times, every expense required a sacrifice elsewhere in the budget. Aside from the books I doubt she held on to anything I gave her during our time together: the pocket camera, the dressing gown in imitation silk, the framed drawings by some comics artist who was popular back then but is now long forgotten. My gifts to her, the act of giving, left me feeling inadequate. I couldn't help but register their cost and how relatively few of them there were. I was clumsy in comparison, suddenly conscious of money and what my lack of inherited taste could mean. Such things usually only existed in the undergrowth of the life we had together; they were things we didn't discuss. There might have been a certain violence to the way she gifted, a triumphant supremacy that was affirmed each time she slid a rectangular box across the table (a necklace with an asymmetrical silver pendant), left a big surprise in the center of the living room (long-distance ice skates, including boots and ice claws), or placed a wrapped, newly published book on my pillow (Tranströmer's *The Sorrow Gondola*), or came home with a box from Gunnarson's Bakery that she dangled before my face before setting it down on the table between our teacups. It was a kind of generosity that cost her nothing, but which she knew I'd never be able to match, and which therefore gave her a secret upper hand. When I ran out of money, she was the one to replenish the fridge and the pantry, and she did it with cheese from the market hall cheese monger, fresh-squeezed juice, and newly ground coffee in brown bags from the specialty shop on Linnégatan. At some point, probably right after it ended, I asked myself if this was what structural violence looked like: to unconsciously teach someone about gifts, where to buy them, how to deliver them. To teach someone that you're not supposed to buy the cheapest pair of pants, ready-made pesto, computer, or frying pan like I'd always done, but that you had to pick the best version? A couple of years later I saw that any notion of latent violence in this exchange was a figment of my own imagination, sparked by the experience of being abandoned and posthumously construed by a mind burning with indignation. Johanna gave me *The New York Trilogy* out of no other impulse than kindness, and the inscription's kisses (which would prefer to be on my lips) were as real as kisses in blue ballpoint on a title page could ever be.

To read with a fever is a lottery; the contents of the text will either dissolve or penetrate deep into the cracks accidentally opened by an out-of-control temperature. This is why *The New York Trilogy* moved me in a way I've never understood, and it is also why I've sought it out today, almost twenty-five years later and with an altogether different fever blazing behind my eyes. *An altogether different fever*, I write, even though every fever is the same fever, with the same nightmares and the same distress. Time folds in on itself, as it often seems to do under the influence of fever, and I suddenly find myself standing side by side with the me from twenty-four years ago. The brink of insanity lies at 102 degrees, but not far below, at 100.4, there's a clearly discernible valley where I wouldn't mind spending my days. In that band your guard drops, and figures from the past are given access, though not as ghosts.

100.4: a temperature where the body's ability to stay alive is intact even as your interest in being an alert and informed social being cools, so as long as you can bear to have the past slinking about your legs like a pack of dogs, this valley offers a pleasant lassitude. I remember the fevers of childhood, all those fevers before the introduction of rapid-read thermometers when taking the temperature required Vaseline and persistence, my mother observing the blue pillar of the quicksilver to confirm what my body already knew: 100.4, a day of soporific dissolution, the walls thin between the world and me. At 100.4 degrees there's nothing in me that whispers "forward" anymore. And isn't that command the truest essence of this world, that which makes everything tick? Forward, forward.

I dropped out of the class that had brought us together before the semester was over. Encouraged and enthused by Johanna, I decided to give my writing a chance and got started on the short story project I'd been thinking about for some time. It was a collection of stories tied together by theme, which might have been successful had I completed more of them. I did make some headway, got at least half-way through or a little longer on all of them, before my courage faltered. Forward is only a direction for people with speed and I spent whole days polishing sentences that were ultimately scrapped altogether. Johanna, naturally, got her degree and landed a job at the local radio station through her dad's connections. Getting home from work around six or seven in the evening, she'd come stand behind me at the big desk and look down at the screen as long as I let her, which I usually did, and then she'd nod and smile. She encouraged me even when the screen showed approximately the same sentences as the day before. I'd never previously let anyone read my writing but with her it was easy—probably because she considered everything I squeezed out with rapt attention. Even though I understood that she was mixing up the kisses on my lips with the appraisal of my work, her kindness still motivated me to keep going. It turned into a game where her advice could be as concrete as the finger she placed on my screen: "let them get each other in the end instead" she might say, or "make her crazier." By the time she came home the next day her will had been done. It turned out that every story required her touch for completion, as if she not only understood my intentions better than I did but as if she alone could see where they might go. I found myself with something akin to enthusiasm for work and managed to establish a routine for my writing, which included reaching a daily word count. There was joy in getting through the rough patches that were part of the effort, and I found that the toil I expended one day would usually be replicable the next day, and the next, and the next. In a few weeks this habit of writing replaced the occasional bursts of inspiration that used to be my main driver but which never yielded more than a few pages at a time, and out of which no more than a paragraph or two would be serviceable at a closer look. I pulled myself together, overcame my fear, became systematic and diligent; I listened to Johanna's praise and suggestions, I wrote again, I wrote better, I kept writing. The despondency that usually plagued me was miraculously gone. I was in Johanna's room now, in a warm and productive embrace. She piled superlatives on top of one another, it was like a campaign, and her words were confirmation that I'd chosen the right path. Afterward, when she'd taken her books and clothes and left me behind in a dusty apartment I couldn't afford and with a collection of furniture I didn't want, I understood that her adoration had tied me to her. Or, rather: it had tied my ability to her. With her, my only reader and my best reader, my closest and most encouraging reader disappeared, and the hurdle to sitting down and finishing anything became insurmountable. For years I tried, consciously and unconsciously and more times than I care to count, to re-create that situation with other people. After Johanna I dated men and women who liked literature but didn't want to read my writing, or who wanted to read my writing but didn't get it, or who got it but had nothing intelligent to say, or who didn't get why I was trying to write in the first place; men and women who enjoyed the wrong kind of literature (crime fiction only) or the right kind of literature for the wrong reasons (Ellroy, because he's hardboiled), or who liked the things I did for the same reasons I did but saw no reason to talk about it, or who simply thought that printed matter had become irrelevant as an art form. None of them could mix the kisses on my lips with anything else. The kisses always landed where they did (on my lips) and never elsewhere in my life or on my attempts to create something.

Maybe it's a coincidence, this sudden urge to reread *The New York Trilogy*, but more likely it's the fever tugging at the nerve that runs up the vertebrae, past the swollen throat, reaching into the space of nightmares and chills. In one way life begins anew each day and every second, but it's also true that I keep returning to the same places in myself. We'd come to worship chance, Johanna and I, like every other couple whose meeting was predicated on it, and that's why Auster's novels were so fascinating to us. I don't think there's any other author who so consciously makes chance an actor in everything.

When we first met, we were both with other people; she with a woman and I with a man who had recently proposed. Happenstance led us to enroll in the same class at the university. I knew I would drop out even before the orientation, but I went to the lectures anyway and sat through the first exam, and when I arrived at the pub after the test, there was only one place to sit. The day prior we'd locked eyes across a crowded lecture hall. Now she was seated at the short end of a large table, wearing jeans and a collarless black button-up. Our wrists began to consort on the table and electrified the event until the wee hours when everyone else had gone home. The Monday that followed we broke up with our significant others in two separate but still interlinked scenes, and the week after we moved into an apartment in Hägersten that a classmate had received in inheritance and was now renting out. I was twenty-seven, Johanna twenty-four. We installed ourselves in each other in a manner that only happens with people who are certain of a long life together, as if we'd received a guarantee that only death would tear us apart. We merged our books and belongings without difference or distinction, and we didn't need to specify that everything we bought (a standing mixer, balcony furniture, a Lars Norén collection titled *De döda pjäserna*) was for communal usage. There was no future plan, no future theater play, no trip, no party, no move that didn't include both of us, and as time went on, the references and experiences we had in common multiplied until they filled our lives to the brim. She was my main character. My life was Johanna; the conversations we had, the place on Earth we shared. I would never again be as sure of anyone as I was of her, as sure that I truly had someone. Not even years later, when I met the dark eyes of my newborn daughter for the first time, would I be as sure that I *had* someone.

During this time, in the mid-nineties, places like Fyra Knop were rare. There was still something unvarnished about the plain wooden table, the man pouring batter onto round crêpe makers next to the stairs at the entrance, and the robust liter bottles of strong apple cider. The space was small and smoke filled, the tables were close together, and the evening was usually late by the time we left, as if time was passing according to a different, more international, clock. The waiter kept a folded kitchen towel tucked into his apron and repeated the orders in French without writing them down, and now and then—in a gesture that was nothing but theater, though that didn't lessen its impact— he'd take the towel and rub an invisible stain on one of the tables. Between six and eleven the doorbell would tinkle incessantly as people poked their heads in, hoping for a free table, and wintertime clouds of steam and cigarette smoke billowed onto the sidewalk every time the door opened. We went there with classmates, hers or mine or ours; we went with my best friend Sally, with other friends, with Johanna's siblings, with some of her new work friends when she'd started at the local radio station. The trick was getting there early to snag one of the bigger tables, and from there on you'd let the evening unspool freely as plates and bottles were introduced and removed, galettes with goat cheese and honey and spinach and crêpes with chocolate and pistachio and brown sugar, and Johanna and I eating from each other's plates like siblings in a way I've never been able to do with anybody else, neither before nor after. We might order a galette upon arrival at six and then two hours would pass before we ordered the next. In that time both the people and their places around the table would have shifted, ash-trays would have filled and emptied, and conversation topics would have emerged, faded, and returned again. Then, at eight or so, we'd order another round of galettes, or crêpes, and the whole dance would start over again. The man with the towel came and rubbed a stain and bussed glasses and carafes and spoke in French with Johanna and others who understood. At the end of the night she and I would sit across from each other on the subway home, the red line from Slussen, still talking. It was like one single conversation that didn't stop even when we were apart, not even the first Christmas we spent away from each other. For my part, the conversations with Johanna lasted long after she left. Maybe they never truly stopped.

It was after an evening at Fyra Knop that I saw the weather change for the first time, the little spectacle I'd later term "the frost." What I just wrote is a lie though; I'd noticed it from the start. Her way of giving me her full attention, only to turn around and answer the phone sounding like she was at an office, or the other way around: the way she sometimes came home, flung her jacket at the wall, and burst into curses over something that had happened earlier that day, only to look at me and break into smile mid-sentence, all within the space of a breath. She had an aptitude for being cold and collected, an ability to change feelings on command. It was a particular kind of talent that had nothing to do with her other abilities. I found her way of turning on and off both admirable and disconcerting. It insinuated that she had that thing known as "full control," which came across as mature, but there was an inhuman bent to it, too, an inhuman temperature. I could easily spend an evening mulling over a single exchange and was never able to turn my emotions on or off. The past never let me go, and I know it was something Johanna found pathetic. "Just drop it," she'd tell me, and I had no idea how. I couldn't choose to hold on to or let go of feelings; instead it would be the feelings that finally gave up and released me.

As we were en route home this evening on the subway from Slussen a drunk and foul-smelling man got on at Zinkensdamm, sat down across the aisle from us, and started to talk to us the way drunk people sometimes do. We wanted to continue our conversation and ignored him. I gave him a polite, slightly dismissive smile, but when he kept babbling, Johanna turned her entire torso to face him and launched into an eloquent, ruthless scolding. I'd never heard her talk to anyone in this way before, I believe the words "shithead," "pizza face," and "piss pig" were involved, and the instant she finished, her expression shifted and she turned to face me again. It was like she'd strapped on and removed a mask in the time it took her to swivel around, but I couldn't tell if the mask had come off or on when she resumed our conversation. I, being sensitive and troubled by conflict, kept glancing at the man while Johanna kept talking to me in her regular voice. I expected her to start laughing and reveal it was all a put-on, or at least comment on the incident some other way, but she just kept talking and the man staggered off at Liljeholmen and the train kept moving. In bed later I said: "I didn't know you have that in you." She didn't understand and looked sincerely befuddled. "The ability to switch like that. With the guy on the subway, you seemed completely indifferent." She laughed. "I mean, I *was* completely indifferent." A smile lingered on her lips as she waited. "You cursed him out like it was nothing, and you seemed no more bothered than if you'd have asked for the time," I said. She shrugged. "So?" I took her hand, as if to soften the words. "I guess I was struck by the way you could talk to him like that and then immediately turn back to me. Like you didn't *feel* anything." Johanna shook her head and let go of my hand. "What are you getting at?" She was no longer smiling. I could feel the temperature drop between us, and I regretted bringing it up in the first place. After this brief episode with the man on the subway, which neither of us ever mentioned again, I understood that "the frost" was part of her—and not as deficiency but as tool, a useful little patch of ice.

I came to the decision to never try to write again several years after Johanna's disappearance and within the span of one minute while I was chopping an onion at Sally's. That summer I'd taken yet another creative writing class without finishing any of the stories I'd started. The other participants had immediately incorporated the teacher's focus on flow into their process and left with folders of completed manuscripts. It was a motley class, open to anyone and populated by energetic seniors and ambitious young people as well as some who had mostly enrolled to drink wine on the big lawn at night—but everyone was happy and everyone finished. I distinguished myself on both counts. The first day I sidled up to the teacher and went in for his approval and praise. He told me that my work had what he termed "a melancholic eye for detail" and something he described as "an inexact precision," and I spent a good bit of time trying to understand what these abstractions might mean until I realized that he told all students more or less the same thing. Their work had "clever distance" or "a disarming brutality" or offered "sunny resistance." Everyone but me appeared to find meaning in these nonsensical constructions. The teacher was an author who had published a handful of poetry collections and novels, and who spoke of his writing in terms of "the magic of creation," "subconscious processes," and "harnessed impulses of spatial presence." At first, Sally laughed out loud when I described him, but then she looked at me, holding aloft the spoon she'd been using to stir a pot of spinach and garlic. "A melancholic eye for detail though, that's spot on." We were making lasagna, my daughter was asleep in the stroller in the hall. I turned on the oven and got a large onion from the pantry, cut the root and the beginnings of a green sprout on the other side. And right then I experienced one of those rare moments where everything is laid out perfectly in front of you: the fact that this was my third writing workshop and I was still stuck; my understanding but puzzled friends; how I'd let others support me; how I'd taken out student loans and bank loans and gotten side jobs in a vain effort to find my way back to that room. I peeled the onion and discarded the rustling skins in the sink, got a cutting board, cleaved the onion in half, and got to work making thin slices. It was suddenly clear to me that this room inside of me had been shuttered a long time ago, at the end of the last century. A simple realization, like seeing the weather through the window: it's raining. The next insight came on the heels of the first and was just as simple, as crystalline: all my writing efforts were a vain attempt to reach for something that was forever lost. The onion was half-sliced, the decision half-made. The third insight presented itself as an image, an expanse that stretched out before me, void of nagging ambition, of any need for ideas. No plans, no vanity. No constant failure. I gave up; I was free. The words for "forgiveness" and "freedom" are the same in several languages; an obvious point perhaps, but in this moment I realized that "letting go" could be said in the same breath. The slices lay perfect in front of me. Sally looked over. "Is that the onion?" She took the cutting board and brushed it all into the frying pan. "Or are you crying?"

Johanna became a person of my past, one of many, and had she not turned into a public figure I'd probably have been more successful in forgetting her. Her memory would have been allowed to fade and only rear its head again during fevers like this one, or during bouts of self-pity and nostalgia; it would have waned and withered until, like a badly restored painting, only a few incoherent fragments remained. Maybe I'd have walked by Fyra Knop and caught a scent linked to a voice. I might have dedicated a little thought to her every time I passed by the coffee shop on Linnégatan, or paused at an article about the laborious making of *The Sorrow Gondola* after Tomas Tranströmer's passing. Like most people who've been abandoned I held the simple hope of never having to see her again; I felt this was the very nature of a separation, and if I couldn't have her all the time, I didn't want her at all, didn't want to hear her name or see her face or anything else that might make me remember her kisses (on my lips). The end itself was a shock; the entire thing was over in less than a week (a love note found in a jacket, peering through the mail slot of a stranger's door, nighttime phone calls, slack-jawed bawling in rush-hour traffic, and moving boxes in too-small trunks), and afterward I spent entire evenings on Sally's couch with wine and coffee, absolutely paralyzed, less capable than ever, and there was only one thing I knew about the future: I never wanted to see Johanna again.

But just as we can't choose our deaths, we can't choose the extension of a broken relationship. Her career was fast and seemingly without limits, as if our relationship had been her springboard. Nobody was surprised; there was something about her that made her well-suited for life in the public eye. She had the gaze, the smile, an entire well of viewpoints that never seemed to run dry. She was able to get her bearings and form an opinion on some topic in the span of one minute—or perhaps more accurately, what passed for "an opinion," and which could easily transform into its opposite at the blink of an eye, like a game, as if the subject matter itself was an irrelevant appendix to the verbal flexing made visible by its light. It was something she'd learned from her family, where argumentation technique was considered much more important than the urgency of the topic, and where every dinner was part of a tournament in rhetoric that had been live for the just over two decades she lived with her parents, and which recommenced every time she came to visit. Her brother and sister were the same, equally quick to dismantle every subject into the sum of its parts. You didn't raise your voice in Johanna's family, you just upped your speed and the number of clauses. I was attracted to it, I inhaled it, I let myself be impregnated by her way of speaking and being. I adapted, made my own version of it, let her change me forever. That's all there is to the self, or the so-called "self": traces of the people we rub up against. I loved Johanna's words and gestures and let them become part of me, intentionally or not. I suppose that is at the core of every relationship, and the reason that in some sense no relationship ever ends.

The truth is that I'd known it from the very start, I already knew it when she got her first job at the local radio station: it was just a matter of time before she'd become a public person. She'd already started doing hour-long interviews on national radio the year before she left me, and I felt like her raspy voice was everywhere, on other shows, too. With time her name became a household name, she was a foreign correspondent for a while and she was photographed at openings and interviewed in magazines and participated regularly in various TV shows. She was considered a highly competent, if not particularly warm, host. This is how our relationship ended: by not fully ending, for me. Her name, which had lived on in a withering little memory box in my head, turned into a name that's now spoken from my radio and TV speakers, a name said with an altogether different resonance, a name that's part of the jumble of famous and semifamous names that whirl through the public sphere accompanied by their faces. Every now and then an acquaintance will ask me, "The host of that show, didn't you guys—?" followed by an expectant smile, by which I gather that they already know the answer and are angling for a bit of intimate gossip. Most of the time I deny the insinuation, and sometimes I'll say something like, "It was so short that I barely remember at this point," and sometimes, "Yeah, but it was very long ago." It would never even cross my mind to offer up an unfavorable anecdote or two. To gossip like that would pitch me straight to the nether reaches of myself. Instead I wonder how Johanna would answer that same question. "I barely remember her" or "It was a really long time ago"—I suppose that's more or less what she'd say if someone would ever think to ask about me.

With time I've come to appreciate her public presence, since something of us lingers in the way she talks. Sometimes she says words that are so familiar that I can hear my own voice in them, like when she picks "skirmish" over "fight," her way of pronouncing the *a* in "baby," or her usage of words like "tumult," "embroiled," and "impoverished," words we found when we reinvented the alphabet together. Only once did I turn off the radio when she was on. I couldn't tell you the precise time of day, but I know it was a Friday evening. It was something trivial, marginal; I must have been the only person to take note, quite like a nutcase who finds private communications in the newspaper, but it was not a sign of madness, at least not when I heard it. It was just a concrete observation. For some reason she was on the panel for a radio show that mixed current events with culture and humor in that contemporary style that doesn't offend anyone, and when a man on the panel recommended Paul Auster's most recent novel, Johanna exclaimed, unbidden: "I've never liked Auster." An abrupt assertion, shot off without prompting, as though she'd been keeping her gun ready and waiting to fire. The point of this statement must have been obscure to the rest of the panel, and it passed without further comment as the discussion meandered on. But I stayed behind with her words. She might as well have said "I've never lived in Hägersten" or "I hate crêpes." Any attempt at making sense of that line would make me sound truly insane to most observers, so I leave it be. A lonely nutcase, a pretentious nutcase with a barren life, the details of which neither Paul Auster nor anybody else would care to describe. And so I leave it be.

2

Niki

There was a time when people who disappeared were hard to find. It's not at all that long ago; many of the now living can remember what it was like to lose somebody for real, to look forward to the next edition of the phone book, to lug it in from the stoop where the volumes had been dropped in a pile, A–M and N–Ö as well as the Yellow Pages, all in a plastic-wrapped stack at thirteen, fourteen pounds. What it was like to plop down on the hall floor and run an index finger down the page in search of the name of someone you'd lost sight of in order to find out if that person might be included this year. Only people with their own landline had their names in the phone book, which meant that anyone who didn't have a permanent address, who lived in a sublet, who had moved to a new city or country, or who simply did not want their number to be publicly available was swimming in the sea of an unregistered populace, and whoever wished to find someone therein had to leave it up to providence. I'd lost track of so many people, for shorter and longer periods of time; there were hours and lifetimes of searching, at times intensively, desperately, for a week or two, sometimes distractedly and sort of chronically over the course of decades. I lost sight of Danne shortly after we entered the Roskilde Festival area and wound up seeing Simple Minds all alone in the crowd that first night. I had to pitch my tent next to strangers and spent an evening fruitlessly wandering around until I happened upon someone from our crew in a bathroom line. The reunion was memorable and the whole incident would, like everything else that summer, turn into a good story, but nothing could compensate for those wayward, lonely hours. A big festival is desolate without friends. And I soon realized that none of my friends, least of all Danne himself, who'd said the unforgettable words "Wait here, I'll be right back," had spent much time trying to find me. In their eyes it was I who'd gone missing. The flier I'd pinned to the huge notice board at the entrance, which was littered with other calls for friends gone missing, was untouched. Now, more than thirty years later, I can't recall what he was going off to do or what I was waiting for or why I finally gave up on waiting and started searching instead, but I remember he told me that he'd gotten high and forgot about me, and that this was the year that I piloted myself out of that crew and sought out new friend groups, people I met at the university, people who did fewer drugs and had more conversations, who kept track of themselves and others.

One of these new friends was Niki, someone I ended up having to search for later on. It was long before I met Johanna, in a first-year English class where Niki and I were in the same seminar. She came up to me and started talking during the first break, and I came to understand that this was how she made friends, simply by hitching her wagon to people she thought seemed nice or who had something about them that appealed to her, in my case a pair of Stan Smiths that were as scruffy as hers. She had chosen her own name, Niki, since she hated the name her parents had given her, and she hated that name because she hated her parents. Whenever she said that word, "hate," she scrunched up her nose and opened her eyes wide as if to underscore that she was on the offensive in her stance. It wasn't some absent-minded, casual type of revulsion she was engaging in, not some kind of residue from punk teenage years, but a fire that burned bright day and night. Despite our many and long conversations, few concrete facts emerged to explain this hatred other than the assertion that these two people were "horrible," so much so that she'd been compelled to move three hundred miles away, change her name, and get a protected phone number. Her claims were shrouded in mystery. I thought the facts would become clearer with time, but Niki's statements about her parents were instead established as truths in their extant and obscure state.

Suddenly I'd joined her circle of many who "knew" that Niki's childhood had been terrible and that her parents deserved to burn in hell, and since I quickly counted as one of her closest friends, I was expected to be loyal and allied with this unverified truth and its want of details. I suppose it made for a certain bond between us, and generally I didn't care what was true or not when it came to her parents; it wasn't the kind of truth that mattered to me. When Niki learned I was sleeping on my grandmother's couch in Jakobsberg, she invited me to share her one-bedroom in the Atlas neighborhood. It was hers through the housing agency, via the quota they had back then for the neediest cases. The category had its own lane, separate from the standard waitlist where I and hundreds of thousands of others languished for decades, and it was intended for battered women with children, people who were severely ill, and others who for various reasons needed an apartment of their own immediately. Niki explained to me that she'd lied and told them that her father had committed incest throughout her childhood and that it was harmful for her to be constantly uprooted. All it took was a certificate from a psychologist and an interview with a social worker, paired with a type of cunning I did not have in me. It was a lie of great precision; incest was a major topic of interest in the late eighties and early nineties. It was debated in the media and discussed at work lunches, and a new crop of experts emerged to testify that incest was a social problem of far vaster scale than anyone had previously realized. Therapists' couches got busy with people whose repressed memories had to be coaxed to the surface. "I'm convinced my dad did it," Niki said when she saw my skeptical face, "even if I don't remember it yet." Niki had been to many therapists of different kinds, but she always seemed to end up at odds with them. All they had to do was question her in the wrong way, or cancel a session, or go on vacation, or talk about tapering off the sessions, and Niki would end the relationship in a rage. A therapist might be amazing one week and absolutely incompetent the next. I realized from the very beginning that this was how she related to other people, that everything was black or white, love or hate, heaven or hell, nothing in between. She picked up two additional friends from our class, they were "brilliant super women," "the world's loveliest people," had "the kindness of bodhisattvas," until one of them reminded Niki to return the records she'd borrowed a couple of weeks earlier. The fact that she said this at a café, in front of other friends, made Niki furious; she'd been "dishonored with the world as witness" by this little rat who she never wished to see again, so when Niki got home that day she tossed the records into a plastic bag, bare vinyl and sleeves all in one jumble, took the subway to the home of their owner, and hung the bag on the door to the building; ciao. The other friend was discarded as part of the same process. But I stayed on, somewhat baffled though mostly fascinated by the intensity of her love and hate, the way she churned through people as if every feeling immediately had to be realized in action. The reasons varied but the method was the same. I must have known I couldn't be an exception to the rule, but at that age (I was twenty-three) friendships were different from the way they are now. They could last forever for two months, two years, two hours; what mattered wasn't time but magnitude, or speed, or the concentrated mass of meaning. Niki touched my heart. Not like the men I sometimes slept with and more rarely fell in love with, but for real, like a soul mate—even though that's not a word I would've used back then—and I wasn't bothered by knowing it would have to come to an end. Niki was an adventure, an endless all-genre drama where nothing was static and nothing could be predicted. She'd tried to kill herself in her teens but said that was all over now, "more or less," and I came to realize that this "more or less" was a way of slashing open a little vein of fear in the people around her, a way of guaranteeing the care of her friends. I never saw her cut herself but I did glimpse a couple of scars and marks. "Anxiety management" was apparently how one of her therapists put it, a vent for the soul in the skin. She made frequent reference to her shrinks, and at some point I thought to ask how she could afford all these therapists in the city, with private practices and different specialties. "They pay," was all she said. "I mean, it's the least they can do." It took me a while to realize that "they" referred to her parents. Today Niki would likely have been given some type of diagnosis for her mental instability, but in the era when I knew her, diagnoses weren't on anyone's mind. Nobody talked about symptoms, criteria, or drugs. People who struggled weren't lumped together in medical communities; it was up to each and every one to do their best to understand themselves and others.

My collected belongings could fit in two bags—mostly books and clothes, as I remember—and I settled down on a mattress in a corner of the apartment's single and unbelievably cluttered room. My bags went at the foot end of the mattress, and I put my toothbrush in the bathroom cabinet and a bottle of Bell's in the pantry. That's all there was to it. My arrival barely made a difference in the apartment's general mess, and what little order I tried to maintain around my bed, the same neatness I'd kept at my grandma's, felt strange and I soon gave it up. My grandmother had worked her entire life cleaning rich people's homes, and she adopted those standards in her own house, too; dusting and vacuuming every week, gleaming stovetops and clean sheets. It was conceivable that Niki's childhood home would have been one of her work places if she'd lived three hundred miles south. Niki's family was wealthy, her parents academics with well-paying jobs, and their house a villa outside of Malmö with a parklike yard. I'd obviously never seen this house with my own eyes, but it had been described to me in great detail, the ground floor which housed her grandfather's medical practice in the middle of the century, its large pocket doors made of oak so thick the people in the waiting room couldn't overhear any doctor-patient conversations. This waiting room had been turned into a kitchen, one of two; there was an even bigger one on the top floor. Niki described the home as eerie and cold, but my imagination was all spacious rooms and large Persian rugs, wall-to-wall bookshelves, lots of bathrooms, and a staircase to yet another floor. I pictured it as impeccably clean and imagined that the contrast to the dirty clutter in the apartment where Niki currently made her home had to be enormous. She claimed that the tidiness of my grandmother's apartment (which she'd seen when we picked up my belongings) was the same as her parents' tidiness; that there was only one type of tidiness, one single way to clean, whereas I argued the opposite: that there were many different types of tidiness, an infinite number of reasons to polish a floor, an infinite number of ways to move across a newly polished floor. "Cleaning is cleaning," Niki said. I couldn't disagree more. Granted, Niki made a point of not cleaning just like many young people who have recently left their childhood homes, but the dirt seemed to touch her on a deeper plane. She loved things most people found gross, and the grosser it was the more she loved it. She was fascinated by the leftovers that sat abandoned for weeks on end in our fridge and liked to take the jars out to examine the contents as they were consumed by biological processes of mold and rot. One morning in July we came across a dead rat in Vasaparken and she crouched over it for a long time, observing the struggle of the maggots in the swollen flesh. It was as if something was perpetually tugging her downward, toward the underworld, the mess, the dirt, and the filth, as if she was unable to feel disgust when others did and was overwhelmed by fascination instead. As if something down there drove her to manifest this dull and sticky filth in her own life, and so she never changed the sheets, never vacuumed, left the dishes in a state most people would find intolerable. I wasn't too bothered by it, though I sometimes missed the blinding whiteness that greeted me whenever I opened the fridge at my grandmother's. There were many ways to clean, and for my grandmother it was about dignity, about getting some of the luster from the homes in which she worked for herself; to me it was a question of adapting, of being able to slide in and slip past without notice. At Grandma's I cleaned as often as she did; at Niki's I never thought to make my bed. A neat little zone in the corner would have looked odd in the tangle of clothes and books and old coffee mugs and glasses and plates encrusted with food and newspapers and records and stuff. I frequently came home to an unlocked door since Niki rarely found her keys when she had to leave; then again it was hard to imagine any burglar bothering to enter the place and look for something of value in the bedlam.

The class in which we met ended, and I skipped the last exam; I took a job at a warehouse, followed by one at Pressbyrån where I worked as a temp and alternated between the different convenience stores across the city whenever someone was out sick. This meant that I sometimes had work and sometimes did not, and on the days when I didn't have work, I stayed at home reading or writing or hanging out with someone, or with Niki. She led a similar existence but wrote more intently and with the explicit ambition of becoming an author. Or rather, to publish a book; she was an author already, she said, since she was writing. Rent was cheap, our expenses were few, and neither of us saw any point in working more than necessary. If we came home late at night, we'd unplug the phone to avoid early calls from potential employers. Now and then I had to spend a long time looking for the phone before I found it shoved into a drawer, the oven, or the hamper. It was common for the device to end up somewhere unexpected when Niki had a call that went wrong, like when someone called who wasn't welcome to call, or the other way around, when someone who was supposed to call didn't. Sometimes she would unplug the phone and sometimes not, which meant it might ring from underneath the couch or inside a pile of newspapers. These things quickly stopped surprising me, just like a knock on the door in the middle of the night followed by

Niki (having lost her keys) stumbling in drunk with a gaggle of new acquaintances and putting on the kettle or getting a bottle and digging up the record player and starting a dance party, or being woken up by her a couple of hours later so we could watch the sun rise from the roof. The roof was an old balcony meant for beating rugs that could only be reached from a ladder in the attic; the hatch was technically sealed but it was easy to open, and once you were through, you had the sunset across the railway tracks and Lake Klara, or the sunrise over the buildings on the other side. We'd drink cloudy homemade wine and scream loud enough to get through to the core of life, believing that there was less in between us and heaven since we were on a roof. Today, several decades later, separated from that time by a new millennium and a new kind of world, I can still understand that scream, perhaps more so than ever, that yearning for closeness and getting to the heart of it all. But I no longer see why we felt the need to climb onto the roof.

The demijohns with the cloudy wine were a project of mine, I kept the slowly hissing vessels in the kitchen and tapped the wine—to the extent that it even deserved that name—in screw top bottles that had been passably rinsed and which I subsequently stored in the fridge. "Urine wine" was the name we had for this concoction, and some batches were so foul that we determined they could only be drunk on the roof, since the view from there compensated for most of the world's ills, including undrinkable wine. *Urine wine on the roof tonight?*, a message waiting for me on a scrap of paper on the table in the morning. *Sure thing*, I'd scribble in response before leaving the apartment, and then we'd meet up in the evening, either just the two of us or with others joining in, to climb onto the roof and let our screams echo between the old buildings. A couple of months after we met, Niki started dating Jonas, a skinny metalsmith and moonshiner who dressed in all black and had done a stint in prison for draft dodging. He let us keep his still in our kitchen, and mash replaced the sugary batches of apple wine in the demijohns. I can still identify the distinctive scent the instant I enter a building, though it's become increasingly rare. The still was a closed, cone-shaped tin vessel with a tube that guided the steamed alcohol to cool above a container where it regained its liquid form, dripped into a catch bucket, and was ultimately purified through a long tube filled with charcoal. This moonshine reached a proof of 40 percent, and its aftertaste brought to mind oily little incinerated animals. Our joint ownership of the still increased the flow of people through our apartment, turning our kitchen into a natural launch pad for all kinds of nights out. People showed up with boxes of pizza that were left behind in piles on the floor, they filled ashtray upon ashtray with cigarette butts before they left, or else they stayed put, lounging on the couch or stretched out on Niki's bed where they'd chat and blow smoke at the ceiling. I met the people who would turn into my closest friends this way, when they turned up in my home out of nowhere, lured by Niki or Jonas and the promise of new people and free alcohol. But as opposed to my previous scene, the drinking wasn't important here. Niki and I were just as happy to spend an entire Friday night with tea, or water, or nothing at all, since what drew us together—and which would from that point on constitute the core of all my relationships—was conversation: a multiyear-long dialogue that began during a break outside a university seminar room when Niki came up to me and commented on my shoes, and which ended a few years later in the echoing stairway of a building in Galway. We could spend weeks apart and still pick right back up where we'd left as soon as we saw each other again, as if only a breath had passed. What I loved the most was that there was never an instant when I knew ahead of time where a conversation with Niki might take me. In contrast to most people I've known in my life she rarely told anecdotes with herself as the main character, or anecdotes she'd already told before, or anecdotes in general, since the nature of an anecdote—beginning, middle, and finale—contradicted Niki's demand for complete authenticity. She didn't care for people who were all pretend, she said; people who altered themselves for others, who interrupted others to talk about themselves, who explained what it was all about, who bragged, who only piped up when they were 100 percent sure, who tried to sound smart, who adopted other people's opinions, who smarmed, who said they agreed when they didn't. Anecdotists were intellectually dishonest, and anyone who made the mistake of telling the same story more than once—about someone being arrested for public inebriation at Hamburg's central station and who subsequently, to their great surprise, woke up sharing a cell with a former classmate; about the grandmother who was more or less on her deathbed when she gave birth to the storyteller's mother; or about the person who had jumped the fence to Visby's botanical garden after it had closed for the night only to discover that the garden's *Cannabis sativa* had no mind-altering properties whatsoever—would not be invited back. Ever since my friendship with Niki I think of the anecdote as a form of chronic illness that attaches itself to some people; that compulsion to tell everything in the shape of a story, to turn life into a formula meant to captivate, impress, upset, or inspire laughter. An anecdote is a sealed box that cannot yield anything other than more sealed boxes until every party to the conversation—or the "so-called conversation" as Niki would put it—sits there with their own pile of sealed boxes, mentally obstructed, tied to the mast, and with the anecdote next in line tugging at their attention. These types of conversations were much like talk shows—*Stop Me If You've Heard This One Before* and whatever else the rest of them are called. We had no TV, at least not in any permanent way, though now and then it happened that someone had rescued a functional television from a dumpster or the garbage room and put it in some corner. None of them were particularly long-lived, but it was in this way I had my first exposure to MTV, an introduction to an entirely new type of frantic publicity, which was initially viewed as offensive but has become the new normal. I remember our amazement at the breathless hosts who were standing up while introducing song after song and the fragmented narrative of the music videos. "This is the future," Niki said. I think she liked it. We didn't watch TV by passively staring at the screen but methodically, critically, as part of a perpetually ongoing analysis of everything around us. To get absorbed by a show, to let yourself be swept up, would have been a sign of mental lassitude. Not even while enormously hungover would we ever have thought to go channel-surfing. TV shows were akin to magazines, political debates, and conversations at family gatherings (she came to a few of mine): incidences of current trends, available to interpret for a deeper under-standing of the world. My relationship to television has barely changed since then; I rarely get absorbed by a show the way others seem to be, I tend to mix them up or forget to watch the next episode, or else I don't catch the title or where it's being shown, and whenever I do find myself in front of a screen my attention is drawn to things without relevance, as if I'm surveying a crowd. I note the ways ac-tors have aged and who's had a face-lift, that the subtitles render the English "billion" as "biljon," a word that doesn't exist in Swedish. TV means that somebody else is trying to control my gaze, whereas books leave me to my own devices. During the time I knew Niki we would spend whole days when we didn't work in the bookshops on Drottninggatan and in the surrounding neighborhood. There were tons of them, each with a different focus, specializing in traditional bourgeois edification or poetry or drama or first editions and similar rarities, or cheap softcovers, or nonfiction. We went shopping with whatever money we had, though we didn't think of these purchases as regular shopping; it was more like a type of towing. We'd say we were headed down to Drottninggatan to "get" some books, not "buy," as if the books with all their contents somehow already belonged to us, as if all we did was provide the bail to set them free and bring them home. But even after they'd arrived in our home, where we read them or started to read them or merely put them somewhere for future reading, we still didn't consider them as belonging fully to us. Just like buying books, the ownership of books was distinct from other types of ownership, more like a loan that might run out or be transferred onto someone else at the drop of a hat, for example as soon as anybody showed an interest in the title or author in question. For a short while I kept *The Man Without Qualities* in the low, blue-lacquered bookcase by my bed, four volumes I'd gotten after someone recommended the novel, but which I'd instantly come to realize I was nowhere near ready for. The first volume was dog-eared at page twenty and lay untouched where I'd put it, until one evening when one of Jonas's work friends opened it. His name was Palle; he'd been traveling the world and was only briefly at home to make some money. He'd taken a welding class through the employment agency and got a job at the plant where Jonas worked, and here he was sitting on my mattress with a cup of tea, sinking into the first pages of this book. He'd skipped the introduction and the translator's note and went straight to the novel itself, which I took as a good sign. The book was his, I knew it immediately, no discussion needed. It had just taken a detour through me.

It's strange that more than thirty years later I'm still able to perfectly recall that blue-lacquered shelf and Palle's face and the cover of *The Man Without Qualities*. The novel has been in my possession multiple times over the course of my life, but it always gets lost, whether in a breakup or by someone borrowing it and not returning it, as if it kept fleeing, arms full of bounty. It's turned into one of those books you own without ever reading, a phenomenon you'll come across in most people's homes: an assurance for tomorrow, a future where you'll have time to read. Wherever you found yourself in Niki's apartment—at the kitchen table or in the bathroom or the hall or sitting on the windowsill— there would be a book by Birgitta Trotzig within eyesight. Sometimes it took a minute of scanning the muddle before I spotted one, *The Exposed* or *In the Time of the Emperor* or most likely *The Marsh King's Daughter*, she owned multiple editions of that one. These were the only books Niki would never dream of giving away or even letting anyone borrow. If somebody happened to open one of these books after finding it by the bed or the sink or on the table, Niki would snatch it from the hands of the person in question like she was taking a box of matches from a child. A list of corrective admonitions would follow. Trotzig didn't write books you could flip through distractedly with the radio on in the background; these weren't books you could stop reading mid-chapter, Niki said, and then she'd read a page or two out loud to illustrate. If the book was *The Marsh King's Daughter*, she barely needed to look at the text; she knew large parts of that novel by heart. She read with a powerful and reverently vibrating voice to ensure that the words reached the listeners and got to our core the way they had with her, shake things up, make things real, blossom, but when the audience's attention began to flag, as it inevitably did, she would stop, offended, and shrug as she concluded what she already knew, that there was very little hope for the world in this question. In my world Birgitta Trotzig is the literary counterpart to the blurred picture you can find on a TV screen. It seems like there's something interesting going on there, but I can't tell what. I turn the knobs, try to change the settings, but the picture remains blurry. For a long time I thought I'd come to understand Niki better, her psychiatric approach to life's spiritual dimensions, her worship of dirt and shame and the pull she felt from the underworld. It seemed to me that the two of them shared a room in a bloodred, severe, and chaotic world I couldn't access, where emotions were the gods that decided almost everything and where anger could result in plates being thrown and where a new passion might entail a journey across the world at two days' notice. I was left behind with sole custody of the apartment. Jonas called to inquire. "No, I have no idea," I said, "I don't get it either." I dove into the blur of *The Marsh King's Daughter* and *The Illness*, but soon returned them to the bookshelf and started cleaning instead. I wasn't ready for Trotzig, and I never would be.

I rarely heard Niki talk about any other profession than that of the author. When P. O. Enquist visited the ABF Building to talk about one of his books (I think it was *Captain Nemo's Library*), Niki went up to the podium afterward and addressed him like a colleague. The two of them chatted for a while. I couldn't hear the contents of their discussion from where I stood by the exit and watched them as the room emptied and Niki took a chair and sat down next to him while he stretched his gangly limbs and listened to what she had to say, smiling and nodding and then adding his own comment. They'd talked about the writing practice, she told me afterward when she stepped out on Sveavägen where I had gone to wait, the importance of being systematic and stubborn, the importance of dedication. In her telling the encounter had been an exchange of experiences and advice between her and the famous author, and perhaps it had been. Niki talked to everyone about everything she was writing. She started on book after book, and each time I and everyone around her were soon familiar with the concept, intrigue, and main characters; we talked about the idea as if it was already a finished novel, as if the book had already been written and was sitting on the kitchen table in front of us, title, cover, and all. The titles in particular inspired long conversations. I remember a few of them. *The Bird Watcher*, about a man and his illegitimate daughter who he kills using his binoculars during a walk in the forest, after which he buries her and reports her as missing. There was also *Basement Girl*, about a child who grows up in a basement and as an adult realizes that her suffering liberates other people from their suffering, and *The Guests of Darkness*, about a girl who grows up at her cruel parents' bed and breakfast, and a family moves in and slowly, assisted by the girl, takes over the business. As far as I know none of these titles ever grew to be more than a title, a skeleton plot, and ten or so intense pages messy with ideas and poignant detail. Once Niki had spent enough time rehashing the idea and the time had come to roll up her sleeves and start writing in a more structured way, for example with the beginning of chapter 1, her initial excitement vanished. The intrigue seemed empty, the characters were flat, her drive was gone. She owned a red portable typewriter and would sit cross-legged in bed, or lie on her back gazing at the ceiling with the typewriter on a pillow by her side, an empty sheet of paper in the platen. She told me I was a "sneaky bastard" who never shared a word about my writing, and it wasn't only a joke. A sneaky bastard who didn't talk even when we were drunk and she tried to badger me for details, some hint of what I was doing in those slender notebooks of mine. In hindsight it's obvious that I was just practicing. I drifted between genres, imitated other writers, and tried to wrestle with what I still wrestle with: the stroll of the thought from the head onto the paper. I knew almost nothing about writing, but there was one thing I did know: for me, the process had to be as tightly sealed as the distillate in the cone-shaped vessel on the stove; I knew that every leakage meant death, that the magic disappeared if I looked too closely, that nothing could be divulged before it was done. In any case it didn't matter, my ideas were trifles compared to hers, and even though I made a few attempts to write intensely and furiously like Niki, I mostly ended up messing around for lack of something more fun to do.

Niki was out of town for a month, her new love looked like James Spader and hailed from the Irish west coast. They went hiking in Bolivia and fell in with some people who served them an herb concoction that gave them visions. Niki said these visions came back to her sometimes, plants crawling across wallpaper and cats sneaking around a corner. Suddenly she was back home, and the phone was given a permanent home in the laundry basket when Jonas grew desperate and took to calling late at night. James Spader had gone home to Galway to participate in some sort of darts competition, and Niki was at the kitchen table writing love letters in ornate script, using the Irish expressions she'd learned. She now had an intense hatred for Jonas and she loved Adrian (who we mostly referred to as James) with the same intensity, she loved Bolivia, she loved Ireland where she had not yet been but where she would soon go, she hated Sweden, and most of all she hated Stockholm, a brain-dead shithole beyond compare. I'd had the apartment to myself for five weeks and was surprised at how much I enjoyed it; I'd slept with Palle a few times, worked, done quite a bit of cleaning, laundered moldy towels I'd found under the tub, cleared the fridge of leftovers whose provenance could no longer be discerned, baked bread, bought real wine, and installed an answering machine. Niki told me that she liked how clean it was, but it took no more than a few days for the apartment to return to its normal state. It was as if she incorporated the apartment into her own chaos, the open suitcase on the floor an epicenter for a new kind of disorder, characterized by foul-smelling clothes and totem figurines and souvenirs she'd bought with the intention of distributing among friends and acquaintances. She gave me a little finger drum, which I put in the blue-lacquered bookcase, and a bottle of clear liquor with a worm in it. She and James had first started talking at Stockholm's Moderna Museet where she'd walked up to him and said: "Why do all these tapes have women's names on them?" and he'd laughed and tossed his floppy bangs and then they went to the museum café and kept talking until it closed. He was touring Europe by train and was set to go on the following day, but plans were made. Anyone who met Niki in passing might get the impression that love was easy for her, a switch she could turn on or off, people who came and went, people she loved and stopped loving. It could seem like a simple mechanism with a narrow register: on or off, black or white, love or hate. In reality it was the opposite: she was an ocean of feelings, with more gradients and nuances than she could handle, as if the full cast of Greek gods and all the emotions and states they represented had been crammed in behind her eyelids. There was an intimate racket in there, never ending. Anything could turn into its opposite in an instant, and with the arrival of James on the scene Niki's world was transformed. She had "always" loved U2, Yeats, Jonathan Swift, Mary Black, Guinness, the color green. Whenever she got a little drunk, she started speaking English, swallowing the endings of the words, in what I assumed was an Irish accent.

Jonas, who I brought up a couple of times since I wondered what had happened to him, was "a controlling asshole" who should be reported to the police. He was uneducated, ugly, manipulative. A little shit, that's what he was, and she'd never loved him and he could take his stinking still and his friends and get lost in whatever swamp he'd crawled out of. When I informed her that Palle had left with the still last time he was over, she looked at me with suspicion. We were at the kitchen table, the tea water about to boil in a pot on the stove. "Palle?" I nodded and instantly regretted having said anything, but I couldn't lie to her. It wasn't just about dignity—my own—and my right to bring home whoever I wanted, but also about authenticity, the straightforward and genuine quality of Niki's and my relationship. "Palle was here while I was away?" I nodded again, and shrugged. This might have been the hardest thing about life with her, the line between friend and enemy, how razor-thin it was. "Why?" she asked. "We slept with each other, he gave me a book, we chatted," I replied. Niki crossed her arms and shut her eyes for a couple of seconds. Her eyelids twitched, it seemed like her eyes were moving fast underneath. A betrayal, I had fraternized with the enemy, and now I was watching Niki process this information. Nothing was settled. Then she looked at me. "What book was it?" The question made no sense, an association in a new, crazy direction, as though she'd received a message from one of her gods of emotion telling her that the title was of crucial importance. *If on a Winter's Night a Traveler*," I told her, which was the truth. When Niki kept looking at me in silence, I added, still speaking the truth: "Wonderful. I read it in one day." She nodded thoughtfully, uncrossed her arms, and smiled at me. Then she got up and went to the stove where she took out mugs and the tea jar. "And then?" she asked. "He came back to get the still so he could give it to Jonas. We had sex again, talked a little. We saw each other a couple of times. But he's left for new adventures now, back to his beloved India." Niki set down the mugs on the table between us. "Did you talk about me at all?" It was a non-chalant question, like a subclause, but I knew it was the most pressing query behind those eyelids, and that each and every one of her hypersensitive gods of emotion was on high alert, ears perked for an insult, a derogatory depiction, any indication of humiliating gossip. "No, we mostly talked about books and the places he was going to visit. All the cities and the beaches. Howrah Station, the art of getting on a train. We talked quite a lot about *Wild at Heart*; Palle said he wanted a snakeskin jacket." Niki added sugar to her tea and stirred, apparently content with the answer. When she was done, I took the spoon from her mug and stirred my own. Obviously this was not the truth, we'd spent hours talking about her. In Palle's view she was unhinged in al-most every conceivable way, but he couldn't give a more specific definition of that word, "unhinged." She was just "fucking unhinged," a description which in the early nine-ties could pass as a diagnosis as good as any, just like "fucking annoying" and "fucking weird" and "just rude." In many ways things were simpler then; these judgments were subjective and based on people's own experience, on what transpires when people come together, but the labels were obscure and mean. "Unhinged"—what does that mean anyway, other than an ability to drive people crazy, disrupting their worlds? She was just Niki to me, and every time I look up at my bookcase, in the region of the letter *C*, and my gaze falls on the well-worn copy of *If on a Winter's Night a Traveler* with Palle's inscription and the little heart still there in pencil, I remember the stale air of the kitchen and the aroma of tealeaves in the pot. I remember Palle's face next to mine on the mattress, his attempts to smoke like Nicolas Cage, and I remember that I began reading when he left that morning and that I was instantly sucked in by the novel's rotating hall of mirrors. Niki's question— "What book was it?"—turned into a sort of proof of her madness, and later I often wondered what would have happened if Palle had come over with another of the books he'd talked about, like Klas Östergren's *Band-Aid* or *Midnight's Children*; if that would have led her irrational madness to explode in a different direction. After a while she took the spoon back from my mug, shoveled more sugar into her tea, and stirred. "Palle huh, are you into him?" A question with no answer since he'd left two weeks prior and was out of reach in a way that's become impossible since then. Letting someone leave literally meant letting someone get lost. Perhaps a postcard would come sailing down onto my doormat, or a letter from some place where he'd been three or four weeks earlier. Maybe I'd send a letter to one of the poste restante addresses he'd given me, to a post office in a city he might pass through at some point unless he'd already done so. Jaipur, Mysore, Delhi. I looked them up in my atlas and tried to remember the routes and the alternate routes, the cities and the possible cities, the beaches and the potential beaches, the islands that were hard to reach, the friends he planned to seek out, some solar eclipse on the coast he was determined not to miss. I made up my own routes so that I could keep track of him, Mumbai, Pune, then south toward Bangalore or Mumbai and the night train up to Rajasthan and onward into the desert, if not Mumbai and then the bus straight to Goa. If I stepped on an A-marked manhole cover, it meant he was on his way to Agra and the Taj Mahal. If I stepped on a K-marked manhole, it meant he was in Kerala. "I might be," I replied. "But in any case it's too late now anyway, right?"

Presumably she got a diagnosis in the end, like everyone else who was "fucking unhinged," "fucking weird," or "just rude," and perhaps she's been through the psychiatric ringer a couple of times with outpatient treatment and drugs and care plans and automatically generated text messages with appointment reminders. Maybe she has a little pill box she rattles every morning, pills that rein in her gods of emotion, and maybe she has regular sessions at a clinic with some bespectacled woman, a registered professional who helps with her self-regard; "So how did you deal with what you felt when he said that?" I've gone looking for answers, for some kind of clue, just as most people have at some point looked for traces of old friends and enemies online, but her name isn't even on the websites that replaced the phone book when it stopped being distributed to the nation's households decades ago. She's nowhere, has no social media, she neither blogs nor posts pictures and film clips, at least not in her own name. In the late nineties I bumped into a mutual acquaintance who told me that Niki had sold her apartment in the Atlas neighborhood when the building was made into a co-op and subsequently moved to another city, maybe another country. This acquaintance wasn't sure, since she herself had been cut out around the time of the move. Niki had broken with Stockholm, had ended it with the entire city and its residents and anyone who'd ever known her there. She'd resolved to never set foot in this shithole again and settle someplace where you could actually breathe. She had reaped a large profit from the sale of the home she'd finagled for herself. I suppose that's what a capital city might offer a "fucking unhinged" person in exchange for what she gave us: parties, warmth, chaos, scoldings, a thousand things to irritate us, and the self-knowledge brought by that irritation.

So how did our friendship end? With a scolding, of course; it was in the cards from the very beginning. All relationships have the potential to end abruptly, it's an inherent risk, but when I became friends with Niki I knew that the brutal end wasn't just one of many conceivable scenarios;

it was the only possible end. I knew with certainty that no friendship survived her, and nevertheless I was surprised. Like death, I guess. Everyone knows it's coming but few look at their living hands and think that those hands will one day go limp and reach room temperature. The whole thing started in the middle of the summer. We were still friends, Niki was going to Ireland, and I was about to move in with Sally, a new acquaintance who had become an instant friend, and who was temporarily living in her dad's villa on Lidingö while he sailed around the world. I was looking forward to swapping the inner city for more space and the forest. Niki was unable to say when she'd be back. "I might stay forever," she said. "We'll get married, and I'll write novels and raise little Catholic children who look like James Spader. I honestly can't imagine a better life." Her packing process was chaotic, with suitcases getting filled then emptied and then filled again. She packed the typewriter and took it out again; she found new arrangements for caviar tubes and crisp bread intended as gifts for James's large family and his friends. I wondered about the odds of the crisp bread surviving transit and wanted to say something about the caviar, how foreign palates rarely appreciated it, that it would fare better in the fridge than scattered across the floor for days on end, but I held my tongue. I had told her about my plans to move into Sally's big house but promised to arrange for another tenant while Niki was out of town. Almost everyone I knew shuffled around between

different sublets, and I would have no trouble finding someone to fill the apartment. "It doesn't matter," Niki said,
"you can stay here, or elsewhere. Someone else can stay
here, or elsewhere." I looked at her. She was sitting on the
floor, had once again extricated the typewriter from the
suitcase. "Well, I was thinking about rent," I said, "doesn't
someone need to live here and cover the rent?" Niki was in
charge of rent and she'd never asked me for a contribution.
During the month she spent in Bolivia I'd been on the look-
out for an invoice in the mail so I could go to the post office
and pay it myself. When it never came, I assumed Niki had
paid in advance. "Never mind rent," she said, "that takes
care of itself. You didn't realize?" She looked up at me with a
surprised smile, as if she was sincerely fascinated by how
dense I was. Did I really not get it? The reason for her care-
less attitude to paid work and the impressive generosity she
sometimes bestowed on me and others. I sighed and trained
my gaze on her luggage again. This might have been the
moment I understood our paths were about to split. "Caviar
has to be kept cold," I said, "or else it goes bad." She took
off a couple of days later, leaving the apartment in the state
it was in, with the rejected parts of her packing strewn over
the floor and the fridge full of caviar tubes. I got a bunch of
trash bags and tossed all the contents of the fridge in the
bin in the yard; I scrubbed the shelves, emptied and discarded everything in the freezer, defrosted it, reserved a
timeslot in the laundry room and washed every piece of

clothing, sheet, and towel I could find; I dried, folded, and organized everything in her closet. I scrubbed the kitchen table clean of crusted food spills and candle wax, bought a pack of kitchen rags and cleaning spray and unleashed myself on the kitchen the way I'd seen my grandma do, hair in a high ponytail and the radio on at full blast; I emptied the cupboards of anything that could expire, collected all the empties and dropped them off at the recycling station, discarded the dead potted plants, and hauled broken plates and cups to the recycling room along with a broken armchair and a toaster that had caught fire. Having cleared the floors of debris, I vacuumed and mopped until the water in the bucket was no longer black. I lugged my mattress to a dumpster on the street, made Niki's bed with clean sheets, hung the key on a string inside the door, and walked away. When I'd scaled the stairs to Sankt Eriksplan, I stopped. Maybe I should write a letter. A note on the table at least, and Sally's number, in case someone were to rent the apartment and needed to get hold of me. I retraced my steps, set down my bags in the hall outside the door, probed for the string, fished up the key and coaxed it out of the mail slot, then unlocked the door. This was a trick we believed we'd come up with ourselves since Niki—and sometimes I—so often forgot the keys and had to wait in the stairwell for assistance. I stepped out of my shoes, located a pen and a piece of paper, and sat down at the kitchen table. The phone rang and kept ringing. The kitchen smelled of cleaning supplies. I wrote down Sally's address and phone number and stuck it to the fridge with a magnet next to a small clipping of a portrait of Birgitta Trotzig with a black middle part and an enigmatic smile. Then the phone started up again. It was on the sofa table. The answering machine I'd bought was nowhere to be found; I suspected Niki had given it to someone. "Hello," a male voice said when I picked up. "Is this Carolina?" Carolina was the name Niki's parents had given her. "No," I said, "I'm her housemate—former housemate." I didn't know which of her names to use. "Niki is in Ireland," I said, finally. The man on the line was her father, his voice dark and smooth. Niki's mother was ill, and she wanted Niki to come home. I listened attentively and tried to picture him; it was Jan Malmsjö's Bishop Vergérus in *Fanny and Alexander*, that furtive anger with the deep roots, the withering gaze and the sharp teeth, but the voice was Beppe Wolgers's soft bedtime voice, curious and interested in her activities: "Wow, she took the train all the way," and "That guy she met, would you happen to have a number for him?" I told him the truth, that I had neither number nor address, not even a surname. All I had was the place: Galway. Niki's father, whose name was Johannes, was quiet for a moment. It sounded like he was chewing on a pencil. A moment later he announced: "There it is." He'd gotten the atlas out, he said, the city was on the west coast and seemed accessible, not that big. We were silent, I could sense an appeal, an offer of sorts. Finally he asked outright if I had any interest in "a little trip to Ireland." I told him I was about to start classes at the university again. "It's still early August," Johannes said, "the semester doesn't start that soon, does it?" I declined as politely as I could, and after another silence he gave me his number in case I changed my mind. I jotted it down in my phone book, and we hung up. Then I left Niki's apartment for the last time and settled in at the ground floor of Sally's house, which was huge and situated just a few minutes from the sea. The top floor was hers. We cleaned on Saturdays, she upstairs and I downstairs, and then we did the kitchen together before we sat down with coffee and baked goods courtesy of Sally. I'd given Niki my new number before she left and was expecting her to call, but time went by without a word from her. The semester started; I dropped out after less than a month and started working as an on-call substitute at Sabbatsberg Hospital, at a ward where the beds were full of old people who were barely alive, and one night I found a woman who had fully died and when I received the woman's son, who wanted to see his mother's body and pay his respects, I came to think of Niki. My employment was at-will, I had no responsibilities, no real plans, and the next day I called Johannes who confirmed that the offer still stood. Niki's mother was more ill and even more anxious to see Niki, and he told me he would send me the money in an envelope. I packed a bag and went into the city center to buy an Interrail card and get British and Irish pounds at the central station, and the following day I was already in my window seat on the train to Copenhagen, studying the railways map they'd given me with a desire to call Palle and exclaim that I too was heading for adventures in a foreign land, look at me, but all I could do was buy a couple of post-cards at Denmark's Hovedbanegården and send them to an assortment of his poste restante addresses. I wasn't sure that my spasms of excitement would still be legible after the cards had traveled by air all the way to India. He'd probably be standing on an Indian street, in the crush of one of those unfathomable crowds he'd told me about, reading my post-card and feeling a Scandinavian breeze pass him by, cold and distant, void of flesh or life. Right, a seat on a half-empty train to Copenhagen, how adventurous. I regretted the postcards the moment I dropped them in the red box outside the station and turned around to head to the plat-form where my next train was waiting. There were young people and huge backpacks everywhere, they were gathered in little groups, some had guitars or cassette players, some had set out little meals with bread rolls and soft cheese and beers in front of them; others leaned their backs against the wall as they slept or smoked or stared into the air with a vacant expression. I took the ferry between Ostend and Harwich in the morning and disembarked at the station in Galway the morning thereafter, crossed the square, checked into a little hotel, and fell asleep on top of the bed still wearing my clothes. When I woke up, it was dark. I sat in bed and studied the city map that the receptionist had given me, trying to figure out how to approach the whole thing. Looking for Niki in a town of 70,000 had been interesting in theory, but at this point it just seemed guileless. I picked up a pen, sectioned the map off into twenty rectangles, and resolved to check them one by one by peering into the stores, the pubs, raking the faces. I had met James only once, on a night in Stockholm the hours before the red-eye for their improvised Bolivia trip. We were on the roof, and he and Niki had compulsively tongued every single moment to destruction, all but moaned through the conversation, distracted by each other's mouths and hands. It seemed like the kind of passion that had to be manifested in the eye of others, a love that blossomed before a witness, and I had to assume that's why I was there, to provide an affirming contrast with my dry and chilly body next to their fire. When the tenor of their kissing changed, I went back down to the apartment. Niki and James came down twenty minutes later, their hair tousled, clearly pleased at having transformed the soundscape of the otherwise sleepy streets, if only for fifteen minutes. I was sure I would recognize James if I laid eyes on him, whatever the odds were for such a fluke. I had promised to let Johannes know when I arrived, but the phone on the room's sole table was dead, and I didn't feel like going down to the reception. Instead I dug out a plastic-wrapped muffin from my bag and drank the last of the lukewarm water from the liter bottle I'd bought at the Dublin station. I showered, brushed my teeth, and crawled into bed. Niki, whose name was Carolina, who I believed to be staying with James, whose name was Adrian—with no address, phone number, or surname. I decided to give it a week.

A methodical approach to an irrational task offers a certain hope of success in a project that is in fact hopeless. And to some extent a methodical approach can provide a sense of meaning, even joy in some cases. This apparent structure might be what makes searching for something so much like writing: the stroll of the thought down to the paper that appears purposeful when it is not; a map with twenty equilateral rectangles superimposed on an unfamiliar town, a quest for someone who is here but has disappeared. I began in square one, which was drawn in the northeastern section of the map and the area around Eyre Square, poking my head into every pub on William Street with random detours down narrow side streets. The remainder of the afternoon unfolded in squares two and three of my map, near the cathedral and the university across the river. The days that followed had a similar pattern; I stuck to my method but yielded to more impulses, hopping on a bus across town or strolling down to Lough Atalia where I walked in the sun along the green by the water. I happened on an enormous library and combed through all the sections. Though it was more or less empty I imagined Niki wandering down the aisles, tracing her index finger across the spines of the books. A large noticeboard with fliers about course books and reading groups and guitar lessons hung by the entrance. I skimmed the messages without a clear sense of what I was looking for until a memory surfaced, a sport called darts. I went inside to ask the librarian if she had a phone book. She stood up and used her full hand to point in the direction of the glass entrance. Outside, on the sidewalk, I could glimpse a phone booth. The book dangled from a metal wire and it was thin and spongy, riddled with cigarette burns. I opened the page to *D* and copied down the address of every dart club listed, as well as one store. The attention required by the search was exhausting, and after dinner at the bar of a Chinese restaurant I didn't have it in me to keep going, so I went back to my room. I began the next day at the phone in the hotel's reception. The addresses for the city's dart clubs were out of date, and the phone numbers either didn't work or had been taken over by people who knew nothing about darts, but I still decided that I was on the right track since it was the only track I had. On High Street I entered a store that sold darts and dartboards, but the owner knew of no Adrian who competed in darts. What he did know was where the competitions took place, and it was there, in square nine on Cross Street, at a pub where dark vinyl couches lined the walls, that I finally came upon James. He was drinking beer with a group of other men, and his gaze initially slipped past me where I stood by the door looking at him, but in the next instant he returned his attention to me with a smile. We hugged, and I squeezed in next to him on the sofa. Niki wasn't there, and when I asked about her, he just shook his head. Everyone had stopped what they were doing and were now watching us with hands cupping their glasses. Smoke floated up from someone's abandoned cigarette in the ashtray. James inhaled and the others leaned in so as to not miss any new detail of this story they'd likely heard several times already. Niki had danced onto the Emerald Isle, literally, jubilant, and she had hugged every single friend and family member of James's, committed the barkeepers' names to memory, taught herself the thorny rules and history of the sport of darts, showed up impromptu at James's work, an accounting firm, and introduced herself to all his colleagues, one by one; she'd learned the city, the city's streets, the city's nervous system and its moods, and thanks to her steady income, meaning the money her parents transferred to her account each month, they soon realized that they could leave James's room at the Shantalla family home for a larger apartment on Sea Road in the town center. The move had been chaotic and interesting, said James; his brother shuttled boxes, furniture, and bags for them in his little car to their new address, where they threw a housewarming party on the very first night, way before either of them had bothered to unpack or get anything in order. Soon enough James comprehended that this question of order had the potential to turn into a problem. The squalor in Niki's Stockholm apartment was one thing; he'd thought of it as a byproduct of our mini-collective's few square feet and the constant flow of people through the apartment, but this was something else. As he unpacked his belongings and arranged them in drawers and closets her stuff remained in bags, or right outside the bags, or piled up on the floor or on chairs where they got mixed up with new purchases, and it didn't take more than a week for his things to get entangled in that mess; he found his shirt with the sleeves cut off in an armchair, the sofa was soon stained with food, coffee, and wine, and the kitchen overflowed not only with plates and grimy leftovers but also with books, papers, records, unopened mail, and drafts of novels. The first two weeks he'd mostly been off work and life was simple, clutter notwithstanding. They spent their days in bed or by the sea and their evenings at a pub or a restaurant or a friend's house. When James went back to work, Niki set up a home office of sorts in the kitchen, hunkering down between piles of books at the kitchen table, pounding on her typewriter while swearing and balling up sheets of paper that she tossed on the floor. Coming home from work James had to start by tidying the kitchen and coaxing Niki, who was getting increasingly frustrated. She said she felt stuck. She yelled that she wanted more from life than this. They made plans to go traveling again, maybe back to South America or on a road trip through the United States, but that required money and so James had to work. Moreover,

Niki was newly distrustful of some of James's friends, all of whom had started out as absolutely lovely people. Now she suspected they were bad-mouthing her when she wasn't around, perhaps rightly so since she irrefutably was an exotic bird with her tendency to let her temper fill every space, to dance when dancing was not appropriate, to be sullen when being sullen was not appropriate; her tendency to find her own emotions unbearable even as she could not imagine keeping them to herself. People who fell in love with Niki fell in love with the very things others were annoyed by, which put James in the position of incessantly having to maneuver and mediate. Like everyone who wanted to be with Niki he became adept at reading her moods. Even before stepping through the door he was able to tell from the sound of her keystrokes whether it had been a good or a bad day. The rest could be discerned from her way of saying hi, ranging from sweet and amorous one day, to offended and growling the next, the prologue to an evening's-long stage play of allegations and suspicion. Niki was far from the ideal guest since nothing about her had the passivity expected by a guest, and though she browsed the library on a daily basis, though she talked to people, learned new things, took an evening class in Irish, life could still feel stifling around her. "I could have done a better job," James said, but his buds around the table protested. You did what you could, they said. You did more than that. They seemed glad that Niki was momentarily out of the picture, even though they agreed that she was brilliant when she was in the right mood. Brilliant and intelligent, educated, thirsty for knowledge, great memory, funny, lovely. That's the kind of night it had been when everything changed; they were at the pub with some friends, throwing darts and drinking beer, she'd been to the library reading Joseph Plunkett, whose poetry she was now reciting, and everyone felt revolutionary and in good spirits when someone stepped into their circle and embraced James. This person was Emily, a woman from his past, and since James had not yet been exposed to Niki's rapport with former wives and girlfriends, he was unaware that they were to be viewed as explosives and made the mistake of happily returning the hug and introducing them to each other. Niki stuck out her hand in hello and managed a smile before she stalked off to the bathroom. When ten minutes had passed and she was not yet back, James went to look for her. She was waiting in between the cigarette machine and the toilet stalls with her arms crossed, furious and snarling, fired up and humiliated, and she yelled at him with all her might. The pub went silent for a second, as if to take the temperature on the crazy, and then reverted to its previous din. "It was the strangest fight of my life," James said, "since there wasn't even a second of it when I knew what it was all about." He looked around the table. "Retroactive fidelity," the man across from him grinned, "maybe she expected you to be a twenty-eight-year old virgin." The guy was wearing a baseball hat turned backward and brought his beer to his lips. The others chuckled. "Hubris of possession and complete subordination, irrational demands on ownership," the man next to him commented. The rest looked at him and nodded. He went on: "It's one thing to be a little jealous of an ex who shows up looking hot, another to make a scene like that." James looked at him, then turned to me. I thought there was a question in his eyes. "Or maybe she was just scared of being abandoned," I said, "catastrophically afraid and catastrophically incapable of handling that feeling." The others stayed silent, someone got up to get more beer. Niki had left that very night; she'd packed a bag and hadn't been seen since. That was almost a week ago. James didn't seem overly worried and had no plans to go look for her. He thought it would only make things worse. I asked if he had any idea where she might be, and the man with the baseball cap told me about a boardinghouse by the river where a Frenchman hosted Interrail travelers and short-term renters passing through. I unfolded my map over the table, and he indicated a little neighborhood south of the river. "Why are you looking for Niki?" James asked and regarded the map, my lines and scribbles. "I need to get hold of her, that's all," I told him. "I don't have an address or a phone number, and she never called me. So this is the only way." New beers landed on the table, and I got up to leave. James wrote down his address and his phone number in the corner of my map. "If you see her," he said. "Tell her hi from me.

Tell her . . ." he didn't finish the sentence. "Just tell her hi from me."

The boardinghouse by the river was a former houseboat that hadn't been permitted to dock at the quay and for that reason had been dragged onto land, where it was also not permitted, wherefore it was once again in the river. The Frenchman who was the boat's proprietor spoke a rattling French-English and let out small rooms with thin walls in the house next door, which he was borrowing from an elderly relative. The rooms cost six pounds a night, which seemed to include the breakfast spread that hadn't yet been cleared, and conversations with the Frenchman himself who was always socializing in the common areas. Niki had stayed there, in one of the big rooms, but she'd vanished the night prior to my arrival since she and the Frenchman had gotten into some kind of clash about something. She'd soured, packed, and left the room without checking out. We were in the garden, he in an office chair that had been rolled onto the lawn. "Sounds like her," I said. He went inside and up a set of stairs with me in tow. The building was a former weaving mill divided into individual rooms with plasterboard. At the center of the top floor was an open kitchen where a few of the guests were currently sitting around a table, drinking beer, and smoking. Niki had stayed in a corner room and standing in the middle of the room I could see how she must have loved it there, with the view of the green hedge, the garden and the water down below, and the large bed, a table, and a reading lamp as well as a private bathroom behind a door in the corner. The Frenchman opened the door, flicked the light switch, and peeked in. "Seems like she forgot this," he said and picked up a bag from the hook next to the sink. It was a plastic grocery bag containing a dirty towel, a wet swimsuit, and *The Marsh King's Daughter* in a beat-up softcover whose pages were soggy from the bathing suit. I left with the bag after promising to get a room from the Frenchman if I for whatever reason decided to stay in the city. "You can have this one," he said. "Sounds great," I replied. In the evening I called James and told him I had sort of run into Niki but also not, that I'd had her in my viewfinder but she'd disappeared again, and I had decided to give up and go back home. Niki might have done the same, maybe she was already on her way to Stockholm and the apartment in Atlas. "No, she's here," James said, "she was here when I came home last night. Everything is fine." I was calling from the hotel reception, standing with the phone in front of me on the desk. The porter was typing away on a keyboard in front of a flickering screen. "Do you want to talk to her?" James asked. "She's in the bath." I checked the wall clock. Half past seven. "No, I'll come over." I still remember the shiny red phone, how my free index finger was wrapped in the curly cord that linked the phone and the receiver, and how the porter glanced my way as he took a sip from his tea mug. Finding her was an accomplishment, a victory, but only for me. Niki had made an effort to escape being found; she'd sent no postcards with her new address and had left no number. Most likely my search would feel like a violation to her, a game of hide-and-seek with someone who had no interest in playing and just wanted to disappear.

The whole thing ended with a scolding in the stairwell, preceded by twenty minutes of biscuits and tea at their kitchen table, the time it took for her to grasp my mission. I thought I saw a shadow float across her face when I told her that her mother was seriously ill, but I might have imagined it. For a moment I'd figured that the facts of the matter, her mother's illness, would somehow trump the fact that I'd betrayed my loyalty in allowing myself to be recruited to hunt her down. I was wrong. "I want you to get your shit and get out of my life," she said, calmly. Then she stood up and raised her voice. "I'm tired, tired, tired." I got the sense that the emotional gods behind her eyes were a little mixed up. She was angry, not tired. We were speaking Swedish throughout and James, who could only follow the melody, put a hand on Niki's arm. She shook him off. "Not you, too," she yelled, in Swedish. I crossed the room to the hall. Niki followed, James at her heels. It was a nice apartment, with wooden floors and door frames painted in various colors and big pots with lush plants in every corner. James and Niki had on the same style of wool sock, whereas I was chilly in my thin cotton ones. I had time to open the door before she fired her last load, which echoed through the stairwell. This dismissal had been part of our friendship from the beginning, the entire thing a walk on perilously thin ice, so I was as prepared as a person can be. Still, something broke within me when I saw Niki's distorted face and absorbed her last words. "You've never been my friend. You bastard. You fucking bastard."

I took the train that night and stepped through the door to Sally's house two days later. I was in the tub when Sally came home. She poked her head through the bathroom door and said hi, waving a bag of fresh chanterelles she'd bought at Hötorget and a bottle of red wine. When the wine was gone, Sally dug out a bottle of cognac. The night turned into a bender, and we took a cab to the city where we danced and were insufferable. I kept postponing my report to Johannes, but after just over a week I called him. I'd hoped to get voicemail, the favored invention for anyone wishing to give a sweeping explanation without difficult follow-up questions, but he picked up immediately. I explained the gist of it, that she'd been found but was not interested, that perhaps I could have presented a more tempting invitation to her childhood home but I'd done what I could. "I'm not sure I understand," he said. "She came. She took a flight the day after you saw each other and she got two days with Sonja." I plopped down on a chair and regarded the garden through the big window. "Sonja?" Johannes sighed. "Sonja is Carolina's mother. She died. It was as if she'd been waiting for Carolina, as if she was holding on until Carolina came home." Johannes was very affable, very serene, a widower who had successfully brought his wayward child home, if only temporarily. When I unpacked, I found the bag with the towel, the wet swimsuit, and *The Marsh King's Daughter* at the bottom of my suitcase. The waterlogged softcover has been in my possession since then, standing in my bookcase. She enjoys regular waves of popularity, Birgitta Trotzig, and whenever people talk about her I always remember the apartment and the kitchen where Niki got onto her feet and yelled for everyone to be quiet while she read to them from *The Marsh King's Daughter*, sort of alone in her worldview but still so full of conviction and ardor. I've always been strangely loath to let anyone borrow this particular book.

3

Alejandro

Right when I wanted a hurricane there was a hurricane. I had longed to be swept off my feet, to get entangled in something, and I had the good luck of getting exactly what I'd asked for, the bad luck of getting everything I thought I wanted, the good luck and the bad luck of having my prayers about passionate love heard. It was not even four months before the turn of the millennium, and I was on my belly in bed next to Kristian in our apartment in Årsta, listening to the little baby campaign that was the culmination of our lovemaking. He worked as a party secretary in the parliament, where he wrote op-eds, speeches, letters from "disgruntled citizens," material for motions, press releases, blog posts for members of parliament, meaning he was a man of campaigns and opinions, his own and other people's shifting opinions, opinions of the future, opinions people weren't yet aware they would soon hold. Opinions were the raw material of his craft, the soil from which the words

grew. Today he is the chief information officer at an envi-
ronmental organization. I sometimes run into him at events
(we have mutual acquaintances), but whenever he sees me
he just nods and looks the other way, as if he wants me to
know: the wound is still there. He was pushing the campaign for a baby ("or two, or three, or five") with one hand
on my lower back and his nose in my hair, abetted by the
fantasies stirred in basically anyone who hears the names
of imaginary future children: Dante, Max, Wilmer, Maya,
Nelson, Lova, Miranda, Berit, Margareta, Julia, Bassian,
Bella, and though it might have looked like a game (Johnny,
Conny, Sonny, Ronny) it was in fact a version of the lobby-
ists' smarmy little bowl of candies in the business fair booth
where it's so easy to pause for a moment, let yourself be
flattered, start chitchatting and joking around, let it slip
that I love the name Frank above any other, and Billy,
which made him laugh out loud, and now the topic was
established and all of a sudden we had a deal. From then on
I felt replaceable, kind of like his opinions, coworkers, and
employers, like a cog or an accessory to the big system he
served so eagerly in his jeans and brand-name blazers and
which was comprehensively analyzed in the thick volumes
that lined his bookshelves, but by the time he tattooed my
name around his biceps to prove the opposite, I was already
on my way out, at that point I'd already had sex with Alejandro in the backseat of a cab from Vaxholm, so in hindsight
it's hard to say which one of us was replaceable in the end.

Alejandro hadn't been invited to join Zomby Woof since he didn't have the requisite competence in any instrument, but legend had it that the night when he impulsively got up on stage and started moving to their music was the first time the band felt complete. At some point someone put a tambourine in his hands, but anyone who saw Alejandro on stage immediately forgot about the instrument he was wielding. He was hypnotizing, you couldn't take your eyes off him, and he moved with such dedication that the word "dance" doesn't quite do it, it was more like he gave his body to the music, offering physical shape to the rhythm without any detours or stopovers. His moments *were* the music in a way I'd never experienced myself and in a way he described, after we'd started dating, with reference to the trips he'd taken on psychedelics where he'd realized that sound and matter are basically the same, that music has an architecture and vice versa, and that our senses, as long as we let them intermingle as they wish, are able to tell us much more than we can imagine. It would turn out that he did a lot of drugs, some of which I'd never even heard of before. The first time I saw him was at Fasching, the band was about to start playing when we entered the bar, he had one foot on an amp as he talked to someone but he turned his head and watched our group find a table, at which point our eyes met. I was with Sally and some other people, we'd gone out, simply out, somewhere, anywhere, looking for music and beer, and we'd ended up at this smoky, familiar jazz club situated in between downtown and Kungsholmen. The others left to go elsewhere after an hour or so, including Sally, but I stayed, as if I was physically incapable of moving. He was dressed in red canvas sneakers, black cigarette pants, a white button-down that he opened after a while to reveal a white tank top underneath, his hair was gathered in a ponytail at his neck, and whenever a song ended the entirety of my being was reduced to the desire for another to start. It was all I wanted, and the sum of me transformed into this cryptic desire, the wish for another song to start. Please, another song, another song with him in it. Zomby Woof played a rhythmic and strange type of electro jazz with two percussionists in addition to drums, as well as piano, synth, double bass, and a trumpet player who every once in a while would get up from a chair at the edge of the stage and fire off a solo. And then there was Alejandro, a front figure of sorts, the face of their only record though he'd barely been present during its recording. It was released as a CD and sold a total of two hundred copies, which tells you all you need to know: the music was visual, improvised, conjured in the present and from the kind of expenditure that is only found in the encounter with a live audience. The musicians in the band were professionals and busy with other projects, so Zomby Woof rarely rehearsed, they played their gigs by ear, meeting up an hour in advance to drink coffee and decide which song they'd start with. That was it, and the rest unfolded in tandem with the atmosphere in the venue, Alejandro's dancing a guide through the show. As the music played he appeared to be fully focused, deep inside himself, but in between the songs he sauntered around the stage, tranquil as he drank water from a glass pitcher, or he'd come up to the mic to say a few words in English, Spanish, or Swedish, thank the audience for their applause, introduce the next song and the band's members, announce an upcoming show. A couple of times I had the feeling that he zoomed in on me when he talked, though naturally I thought it was just my own imagination, unless, I thought, that belief itself was just my own imagination, which turned out to be the case, because in announcing one of the last songs he said, "This is for the lonely lady in black," and pointed straight at me. I raised my hand and waved a little in response. Our relationship had begun.

Sally and I often had nights like this when we just went out on the town; it could be just the two of us or we might make some calls to people who would join us as the night progressed, not looking for beer or music or conversation with all these strangers we kept running into but rather the feeling of a certain kind of freedom, and if we'd been other people who lived elsewhere we might have gone fishing in search of that same feeling, we might have jumped naked into the ocean and ended the night next to each other on a rocky beach, gazing at the horizon. A couple of years prior her dad had disappeared on a sailboat in the Pacific Ocean, and during the year or so when nobody knew where he was, when it was still conceivable that he was alive, we were always at a bar or a restaurant contemplating that possibility. There's no better place for hope than a bar, especially when hope is in short supply. When this year or so was coming to an end, she could no longer be left alone; if she were, she would end up at home with a map and thoughts about the ocean wind and the way it turns in the Philippine Sea and the water's movement at a straight angle from the wind, which means that a ship will drive north when the wind is western, and the subtropical ocean gyres that forms in those waters, just north of the equator. At Fyra Knop there was no wind, nor at Fenix or Indigo, where we liked to eat soup at the window table and where we went when the body was found and shipped home, and where we gathered after the funeral. This, however, was a Wednesday night and I had left Kristian in bed and biked through the drizzle to get to Sally's; we'd had tea and wine and made some calls. Some people had gotten cell phones at this point, but others had not. Some had voice mails at home that they would call and check for messages. There were others who had been given a cell phone through their jobs, and they could use them to make clandestine personal calls. At least one person had an old beeper, which chirped and flashed. Sally had sold her father's house on Lidingö about a year earlier and bought an apartment on Malmgårdsvägen that had space for a workshop where she upholstered furniture for people who wanted to give new life to their old armchairs and chairs and couches. I was sitting on a discolored stool with sharp nails dotting the perimeter of the seat, a work in progress. Sally had on carpenter pants stained with paint and glue but was about to go slip into something else. Early on in our friendship we'd explored the possibility that we were in love, but those feelings had soon subsided and made space for something much more enduring, a multiyear conversation that went round and round, a true love without claim to ownership, a bracing pact in the face of every new circumstance in our respective lives. During the years we'd known each other, I'd cried on her couch more times than I can count, the furniture changing but the crying staying more or less the same; I'd laughed and been in love, been ugly, jealous, a failure; we'd come to braid our lives together like it was the most natural thing in the world, with a tacit and mutual promise to protect each other; if I could bring only one person to a deserted island, and so on. We were at the kitchen table; Sally was scanning the listings in the newspaper, a calendar with picks for events and shows. *"Freaky bamboo jazz with a dance surprise*. What do you think?" She slid the paper my way, left for the bedroom, and emerged in something that looked like a summer dress. "It's almost October," I said. Sally shrugged and pointed at me. "How about yourself, attending a funeral per usual?" We left the apartment and took the bus to the venue, where we bumped into a couple of people we knew in line. It was eight in the evening and because my life took a turn just a few hours later, in the moment when I, without even a hint of hesitation, knocked on the door to the unspeakably smoky room where the members of Zomby Woof had retreated after the show, I can now recall everything that occurred in the preceding hours with a strange clarity. The wet asphalt on Kungsbron, the gaggle of teens outside Burger King on the corner of Vasagatan, Sally pulling out the antenna of her cell phone with her teeth, saying, "Let's fucking move," since she was so cold in her summer dress under a thin blazer, and these details now appear so pedestrian and naive to me, I seem so innocent and distracted, as though there were no seminal events left for me, no cataclysmic decisions to make, as if I was already done with everything in my life that might burn.

Up until that evening I'd always maintained that humans are basically rational, that behavior in general is motivated by calculations, whether simple or complex, conscious or misguided or inscrutable, but calculations nevertheless, and that there's some kind of intention in there about reaping, or advantage, about happiness, pleasure, joy maybe; that there's a kind of will humans are pretty much set to follow since they are basically wise, since they seek the best for themselves and sometimes also others. But when I knocked on that door, regarding my own knuckles—which were dried and chapped from the fall weather but warm from the night—next to the handwritten sign saying *backstage + crew*, I realized I'd been wrong, that it is only after the fact

that we attach those calculations to our impulses, to the
mad wild dogs that actually run our lives. I'd sat in Sally's
couches and armchairs, on the roof of Niki's apartment
building in Atlas, in the break rooms of various places of
employment, in campus cafés and in many other locations,
acting out my role as an apostle of reason. Niki liked to say
things like "history proves that mankind is absolutely insane," but there was not a single time I agreed with her.
Instead I argued that to the contrary history offers evidence
of man's rationality and good sense, even good intentions.
These discussions were theoretical and general, banal maybe,
but my conviction that humans were reasonable made life
easier. It made me good. It made me whole. It kept me away
from the chasm of darkness. The day after Zomby Woof's
show at Fasching I wanted to call Niki and everyone else
and tell them they'd been right. Sitting on the subway on
my way to work (I edited course books for an educational
publisher in Solna) I watched the faces of the strangers
around me and saw, for the first time, that which some
chaos theorist had termed "the collection of unpredictable
variables," a kind of wild and everlasting insanity right
beneath the skin of every single person. I had to assume it
had been there all along, just that I hadn't seen it. Nothing
happened that evening—"happened"—but when I stepped
through the door and entered the room, Alejandro looked
up as if he'd been expecting me, and a few hours later we
said goodbye with a sense of mutual understanding that

didn't need to be put into words. The family on his mother's side had been massacred in Sobibór, his dad had been interned at Estadio Chile with Victor Jara in September 1973, the dance hailed from Stockholm's Balettakademien and some British dance company, but it had always been in his body, and what he told me, the *information* he shared with me, I carefully committed to memory with a view to recounting it to Sally and others who might ask, and perhaps also for the benefit of future me, but the *information* was just the container and not by any stretch the *details* that woke me up the next morning, heart thumping, next to Kristian and in the midst of our neat life with his thick books on the bedside table, all of them with terms like *organizing* and *globalization* in the title. I was back on Sally's couch that evening. The couch was old and soft and belonged to a client who hadn't picked it up, it was upholstered in a new red linen cloth patterned with purple flowers that had no referent in the real world, they were simply *flowers*, a human fantasy about flowers, the kind of freedom artists have when it comes to nature, to observe it and then choose to invent something else instead. We drank tea and ate grilled cheese sandwiches with mustard. "Victor Jara?" I nodded. "Sobibór?" I nodded again. "And what did you talk about for three hours?" Sally and I sat next to each other by the long sofa table. A movie, *Happiness*, was still in its case in front of our plates, but we waited to put it in the VCR. Our movie nights often went like this, the film left untouched. I shrugged. I honestly had no idea what Alejandro and I had been talking about, I just knew that I'd inhaled him, the dancing was still in me, the way he moved, the red sneakers that were so nimble over the floor, the folds around the corners of his mouth that multiplied in parentheses when he smiled, his way of talking which was a stream of unsorted sentences and associations and questions all probing in a direction Kristian would often dismiss, in English, as *beside the point*. Maybe this was where it would all play out, from now on. I considered that maybe there was no place I'd rather be than in the details next to all this *information*, all this surface. I wanted to sink into Alejandro, that was all, dive deeper into us, even as I didn't know what I would find there, and when I thought about his hands undoing and remaking the bun at his neck there was a tremor, like I was shook by the very existence of those hands, the fact that those hands were attached to him and followed his brain's commands, that this whole person was alive and had been moving through the city while we were ships in the night, that he'd been on some street or home in his bedroom, that he'd been somewhere, that he'd been somewhere all this time, that any of it could be allowed. Most of all I wanted to start the film, curl up on the couch, and wake up in time for the credits covered by a blanket Sally had spread over me, just like I'd done a hundred times before. I felt sick, feverish, like my insides had been restructured, the organs slotted into new places and my thoughts exchanged. My relationship to myself, this "self," felt oddly loose, as if the smallest tremor might cause my life to cut loose from its tethers and sail into space. Sally picked up the movie case and read the blurbs without enthusiasm. "When are you going to see each other?" She returned the case to the table. "I don't know," I said. She gave a little laugh and went to bring our plates to the kitchen where she rattled around for a while before she came back with the teapot newly topped up. Then she crouched in front of the VCR player, slid the movie in, and sat down with a remote in each hand. She fast-forwarded past a trailer, pressed pause at the title sequence, and turned to look at me. "Saturday," I said.

Everyone I know remembers the time right before the turn of the millennium with a certain embarrassment since the excitement seemed so disproportionate after the fact, so headless; silly, in a way. It was a collective impulse, like a global popular movement, but nobody could give it a more profound explanation than "the passing of time." The numbers felt magical, and they *were* magical, but only in the way that numbers are. It must have been all the zeroes, and the hope that they were on the other side of a purifying fire, or the belief that a number as even and perfect as 2000 had to be proof of something, a triumph in and of itself, evidence that man was the master of time and not the other way around. Lists were made, thousands of lists that chronicled the century, the millennium, perhaps as a way of tending to the memory of it all, but above all to get rid of it with the expectation that the past would disappear if only it was categorized comprehensively enough. Earlier, when I was a child and a teenager, the new millennium had been a glowing beacon in the distant future, a place with a glittering number two and three fabulous zeroes, where I would be an adult and carry myself without doubt. Over the course of the years, ever since the early 1980s, I had made plans with lots of different people for midnight of the new millennium; I was to meet Katarina and Anette at Dejegatan's soccer fields, Jimmy Pihl at Brandenburg Gate, Laura and three other Americans whose names I've forgotten at Cape Comorin, and, of course, Danne at the dive bar Kvarnen, pacts made in a state of fleeting elation or while high on the future, in a sort of arrogance vis-à-vis the passing of time. When the day finally came around, I had no intention of showing up at some predetermined spot and I doubted that anyone else did either, except for Danne maybe, who I would often bump into around Kvarnen and sometimes we'd chat for a while; he seemed to be drunk or hungover most of the time; he wore a green-white scarf if it was game day and told me that Afghan hashish had the same inflation sensitivity as Big Macs. The two of us had chosen different paths in life but seemed to follow similar routes in the city, and every time we ran into each other there was a slight sense of discomfort in my gut, around my solar plexus or wherever my alternate lifestyles might be located, an awareness that I could have ended up standing next to him with the price of hashish and home games on the agenda. Then I saw that he viewed me with similar pity, my compliant maturity and the middling career and the relationships that didn't quite last, constant moves and no kids. Danne had three of them, with three different women, three different "mean women," but he didn't seem particularly involved in family life of any sort nor, as far as I could tell, in any sort of steady work life. He saw the kids every now and then, went to Roskilde or some other festival if he had the money, and was feeling "fucking good about life," and a new millennium was nothing to worry about. "Time is all in here," he said and tapped his skull with a finger, "nothing to get in a tizzy about." As for me, I had looked forward to the new millennium while it was still remote, a gift that was marvelous while still wrapped, but the closer we got the more ridiculous my fantasies about myself as an "adult" at this point in the future looked. We probably all shared that sentiment when it came down to it, that the gift wasn't a gift, just another day in our lives that would come and go like the rest of them. Some of the anticipation stemmed from the concept of a bug in all the world's computer systems, a bug that was prophesied to wreak havoc and create an atmosphere of disaster. Others talked about a timed space invasion, but the majority just wanted to party, long and deep and hard, they wanted to attend the mother of all parties, the mother of all parties' mother, they wanted to be able to tell future generations that Y2K was such a wild *party*, and even if that did not ultimately describe the evening they would still talk about what a wild party Y2K was. Sally wore a pin with *1900* encircled by a heart, the only slogan pin I've ever seen her wear, but she'd nonetheless started to try on dresses. The movie was over, I'd fallen asleep in the middle of it and woke to the credits, and now I was cradling my cold mug of tea and was expected to have an opinion regarding black or red, long or short, understated or gala. The plan was that we'd have time for three events over the course of New Year's Eve: a pre-party with dinner, a midnight party, and an after party. "Three parties, three dresses," Sally said. We'd host the dinner party. She had spent a couple of days combing through the city's secondhand stores and as a result had acquired a pile of dresses she was now exhibiting to me, her audience. Sally loved clothes and owned several hundred garments. There were nights that consisted solely of her changing and changing so that we never got going and stayed home with clothes and charades instead, or clothes and reading to each other (Kristina Lugn's *The Dog Hour*, Sonja Åkesson's *Domestic Peace*) or clothes and wine. Sally was never in a relationship, she just had *lovers* who came and went, or rather came and were booted, and usually it was over before it had started. It was a game for her, or at least she pretended it was a game, a bedroom farce in which she forgot the men's names and laughed at their attempts to snare her. She was interested in sharing her life with someone, *in theory*, in the future, at some point when the right person came along. But whenever the right person did seem to have come along, an unmarried man her age with a nice character and whom she found attractive, he was still not the right person in the end. "Picky," a word that might perhaps be used for her, but her approach wasn't picky, she wasn't discriminating or fussy or even scrupulous; in fact, it wasn't any characteristic of hers that led her to show the men the door the minute they settled in and cautiously placed a toothbrush on the sink. Instead it was the emptiness where a characteristic should have been, if trust is a characteristic, since things started to get shaky for Sally the moment she was about to get attached to anyone. "Getting stuck," she called it, while I called it "getting attached," the distance between these two concepts a cornerstone of our conversations, her fear of "getting stuck" and my tendency to "get attached." Her current lover was a safe bet, Robert was about to return to Tel Aviv and his studies in medicine or chemistry (she could never remember which) and might write her a thirsty email or two before giving up. When I asked if she planned to visit, she just frowned. Trust, after all, is only a word when you can't feel it in your body. As soon as trust attaches, as soon as it takes root, it fuses with the rest of what's there, takes on other names. Johanna, Hägersten,

Dad, Atlas, Farsta. *Getting attached*, to me they were like tattoos, everything and every detail present and intact, everyone I'd loved and liked was still with me. I watched as Sally put the dresses she had already tried on hangers and transferred a stack of them to the closet. She'd picked three and selected three runner-ups. *Getting stuck*. Maybe it was just about the right dress and the right sort of high, the timing of stumbling into the right person in a moment when your boundaries happened to be a bit loose so that trust could attach itself even when it could not, like that indestructible marble egg that would explode if you struck it at the exact, magic hour.

So that Saturday then, it was in Vaxholm at a venue with a winterized veranda that looked onto the quay, Zomby Woof was the second of four bands and stepped off the stage right before nine, after which he wove his way to my table by the window. I was solo, sober, alert as if the rest of my life hinged on these moments; I tried to achieve a state of wakefulness that was more than awake, a sort of absolute tension, senses wide-open. I felt void of history, as if I came from nowhere, as if the twentieth century had not happened in me for thirty years already and was now coming to an end, and when we stood up a couple of hours later we had not touched more than this: his index finger had at one point caressed the back of my hand. A few millimeters of skin touching for no more than a fraction of a second, but today, more than twenty years later, I can still recall the way it reverberated, how my blood no longer fit in my veins, the way my life no longer fit in me, the way it spilled over and stuck to everything else, already in the cab home and then at his apartment, several hours, a one-bedroom in Örnsberg with a narrow bed in a corner where our laughter ceased and was replaced by a gravity so demanding that it scared me, because it was no longer about pleasure but about something more fundamental, a room in me where everything was spacious and available, my childhood, my people, the connections between everything. "Desire" seemed like "desire" until I disappeared inside of it and stayed in there. It made a different kind of desire appear, an agreement about temporary magic, when places in us that could not touch did touch. To be permitted authenticity in the midst of this act, with not a single thought in my head, without imitation, to be permitted to wreck my life in peace once more. I was so close to myself in situations like this, right at the edge, but to find him there, in my own flesh, the fact that I was an introvert and still found him there, as if we'd always waited for each other and the sweat and the flame that became ours so fast.

The morning after he was up way before me to "do something" in the city, but the next time I woke up he was back by my side and I slipped out of my dream without seeing the edge where the dream finished and the day began, or the edge where "I" began. This is how I remember Alejandro even today, absolutely still on the pillow, with his face right close to mine and his black eyes like a colon I could zoom in on and press through. I've had more than my share of magic in life, most often in the encounter with others. There is something there, and *only* there. I can't be more specific than that, can only say that if we're searching we should look in each other, that a pair of eyes are another's sideways colon into something, or out of something.

"A messy guy," Sally said before even a week had passed, two of her fingers scratching on either side of "messy," that word, a teenage quality some of us never leave behind. Today this "messy" might have placed him on a point on a medical spectrum, but it all happened in October before the turn of the millennium. Sally helped me move from Årsta. Kristian tossed the last of my belongings out through the window, a box of clothes and then the hangers came sailing down, one after the other. When I understood that he was trying to hit me, I went to stand next to the building wall and waited there until I heard the window slam shut. I hauled the boxes up to Sally's attic studio and dragged a mattress into her workshop. "A messy guy," and this wasn't in reference to the drugs but his way of coming and going, the way he'd disappear and then call from another town two days later, the way he'd show up much later than the agreed time, or much earlier, or not at all. He lived without plans and promises and without any sense of the future, he was afraid of "the terrorism of the everyday," whereas I was helplessly attached to this everyday, the precise hours which pass in us with such care, the detailed plan for the aching miracle, which meant that the end to the story was perfectly visible from the start, a premise given in advance. It was the nature of it that it would be over, kind of like a season, and I suppose that's exactly where we found our fire. "We led different lives, that's all," my standard response to anyone who asked what happened between us, even if "different lives" was polite and "that's all" a straight lie. He was a messy guy in a tidy world, constantly in motion and defined by polarity, and then I'd add, "It would never have worked in the long run"; a qualified guess, sure, but above all an attempt to make myself feel better.

The first of Sally's New Year's dresses was long and blue with a thin golden trim and a bold slit up one side. The slit, too, had a golden trim, an eye-catching *V* turned upside down, which together with Sally's pronounced collarbones and frequent, boisterous laughter, set the tone for the night ahead. Sally was bigger than me, taller especially, but I'd borrowed a black dress from her that she'd taken in so it would fit me. It was perfect. Nothing came out of her hands less than perfect, she extended her care to every physical object in the world, and whenever I arrived at a party I could immediately tell if she was there or not because her shoes would be neatly parked on a shoe rack or in a corner next to the muddle made by everyone else's shoes. There was an inherent pleasure to her hands and movement, a tenderness for objects of all sorts, and objects, in turn, seemed to come alive through her. When she told me that the carbonator she'd been gifted by a customer was really ugly, she made her voice quiet so that the machine wouldn't hear and be upset, and when she placed it in a cupboard that was already occupied by a plastic coffee maker and a microwave and some other ugly kitchen tools, she did it with the same type of care and methodical devotion that she displayed when repairing furniture or caring for her father's grave, a constant respect for every detail of physical life. The dinner party was at her place, about ten guests around a long table in the living room and another table next to it set with wine and bubbly, people smoking under the fan and on the building's stairwell balcony; the main course (baked salmon) was delayed and the dessert (sorbet) rushed since we had to get to our next destination. Sally was sitting in the kitchen smoking a cigarillo with one foot on the table, the slit revealing the length of her leg. She was about to go change in the bedroom. She blew smoke in the direction of an open window. "Okay, so I have just three wishes for this coming decade," she said. "For myself, I mean." I was more sober than she and was trying to clear the table of plates and food before we had to go, stacking plates and cutlery in the sink, putting wineglasses on the counter and empty bottles in bags. We'd planned the dinner thinking we'd always come to remember the faces around the table, imagining that the occasion alone would make company and conversations memorable, but in hindsight I can only recall a fraction of the guests, Sally's brother Jack who lived in New York; Beth, his girlfriend at the time who spent the dinner casting long glances my direction and later that night tried to kiss me on the dance floor of Södra Teatern; and Markus, Sally's childhood friend who was already at that point a famous director, as well as Paul who was sitting across from Markus and made a point of pretending not to know who he was. We had the entirety of the twentieth century behind us and an unknown millennium in front of us, an epic split, and still we gave ourselves to small things, corrupt feelings. Paul who said, "What's your name again? Rasmus?" and Markus who corrected him, offended, and Anna, a journalist, who said, "I know who you are, I've seen a ton of your stuff," and told us about an amazing play she'd seen that Markus had not directed, and Markus who corrected this, too, and shortly thereafter got out his phone and started making calls to find another party. "Three wishes, that's a pretty modest list," Sally said with a demonstrative drag on her cigarillo, an imitation of a drag with the cigarillo between two straight fingers. Only people who smoke once or twice a year smoke like that, they "smoke," intensely communing with the mannerisms of smoking, demonstratively displaying their freedom. Sally tossed her cigarillo in the sink and stood up so the slit closed around her thigh and the dress was once again slim and perfect around her. "Peace, kisses, and a baby. Is that so much to ask for?"

Alejandro had left the night before, he was heading to Latin America with "a couple of touchdowns in the United States on the way there." He asked to see me, and I knew that this was going to be the end. For the first time I broke into tears and I took a cab to Örnsberg, not in order to stop him but just to look at him, and we were standing in the hall and he put one hand on my chest and the other on his own. It was over and we didn't even need to speak it, we didn't need to bring order in the semantics around "together" and "apart," I didn't need to ask when he was coming back and be unhappy about my own pushiness, and he didn't need to wriggle out of answering or break any promises. The end would be as natural as the beginning. But then he looked at his watch. "Four hours until takeoff. You can go get your passport." All I could do was stare at him. "What do you mean?" He lay his hands on my shoulders but said nothing more. Later that night we went our separate ways in the big atrium of Central Station and with my hands in my pockets I slowly walked toward the Vasagatan exit. Each time I turned he was standing in the same spot, looking at me. It was probably his certainty that I'd say no that allowed him to ask, a way of making the end well-defined and mutual, easier for both of us to bear. Our relationship was the length of a breath and yet he stayed with me, as if there was something in me that bent around him, a new paradigm for all my future verbs. Everyone I've loved or "loved" since then has had no alternative but to accept being measured against him during a few inescapable moments in the early stages, and I've had to loudly clear my throat to boot those thoughts, since they've been both irrational and unjust in every case, and since the outcome is never to the advantage of anybody else. My daytime self can, in the company of acquaintances, describe Alejandro as "a grand trifle," but there's a recurring dream where he knocks on my door and asks if I'm coming, and I never hesitate, I just take my coat and follow him. I don't even look back.

Sally slipped on the second of her dresses for the evening, a black, sparkling tube that clung to her lines from armpit to knee and had two thin shoulder straps, while the taxi down on the street got tired and left. We'd had the radio on all day, with reports every hour from a new place on the planet where midnight had struck, and the beauty of this rolling turn of the millennium was remarkable, that we lived on a spinning globe in the light of the sun, which came and went over the horizons, and now it was almost our turn. I'd splashed olive oil on my dress while cooking and Sally lent me a pair of dress pants and a black button-down. Then I gave her a ride on my bike between the snow drifts on Katarina Bangata and Östgötagatan before we walked the last stretch up the hill to Mosebacke Square and got in the short line to Södra Teatern. We had bought the tickets back in August. Jack and Beth were arguing in a corner by the coat check and Anna was in the crush of people at the long bar, which had been decorated with twinkling string lights. A bottle of sparkling wine was included in the cover. "Kinda gross, honestly," Sally said and put the bottle to her lips. I waited for the bartender who gave us the wine to hand me a glass but nothing materialized. When I scanned the room, I realized that everyone was rubbing shoulders while sipping straight from their own personal bottle. It was drawing nearer to eleven. Jack left the party and returned twenty minutes later. During that time Beth asked if it was true what she'd heard, that I'd dated that TV host, "the hot one," and I shook my head. A moment later I said, "I believe she's on the radio, not TV," at which Beth laughed, "See, I knew you knew her!" The DJ took off his shirt, cranked the volume, and yelled into his little microphone. People had started to gather on the terrace outside to get a good spot. Some had brought pocket cameras and were photographing each other and themselves against the backdrop of Slussen, the Old Town, and the sparkling stage erected on Skeppsbron's quay. You could already hear fireworks and firecrackers going off, there were groups of people moving about all over the place and the snow that had fallen during the day had stuck around in the freezing temperatures, making everything white. Jack was dancing with Anna and Beth, and Sally joined me on the terrace. "For a few strange hours," she said and looked out over the banister, "the two of you will be on the same Earth but in separate millennia." She drank from her bottle. "I thought about that, too," I said. Sally slowly nodded. "Which shows that time, in and of itself, is just a construct," she continued, "this whole silly business." She gestured at the sky with the bottle in her hand and raised her voice, "Everyone can go home," she shouted, "it's nothing but falsehood and trickery, this whole damn thing." A few faces turned to look at her but nobody cared all that much in the midst of the clamor and the music. "Maybe you should slow down a little with that," I said when she put her mouth to the bottle again. I'd set mine down somewhere and had no plan to go find it. People who wanted to be outside for midnight were pressing on from inside. The spectacular view was what they'd paid for, parquet floors under the evening sky and the city's fireworks, operated by contracted experts. This little perch on the northern edge of Södermalm would also be a good place to watch darkness take over if the Y2K bug did hit, or if something more unexpected happened, for example if the universe decided to roar and swallow us up, or if the zeroes in the year 2000 were to be delivered along with a message of some sort. I saw Beth and the others push their way toward us through the throng. On the opposite side of the terrace was Markus with some other people. It was fifteen minutes before midnight; the racket of firecrackers going off became more frequent, and a couple of glittering fireworks exploded from behind the buildings on Katarinavägen. It was cold, I was freezing. Once Beth and Jack had made their way to us Beth raised her bottle in toast and Sally lifted hers, then took another drink. "At long last this fucking millennium can begin," she said. We were standing close together, squeezed by the crowd. "Yeah, finally we can forget and move on," I said. Sally laughed as if I'd made a joke. "Move on, sure," she said, "but forgetting has never been your thing."

I never saw Sally's third dress of the evening since I left the party after midnight, went home to Sally's, and fell asleep on the mattress with earplugs in, but the dress was red and made from stretchy viscose, and it tore a few hours into the new century when she straddled a marine biologist in a bathroom. It was at an after party along the red subway line north, Sally didn't remember exactly, but she did find a phone number scribbled with her own lipstick on her wrist. On the morning when all of Earth's midnights had finally passed and the planet was hungover and content and ready, Sally and I were drinking coffee and eating filmjölk at her kitchen table. "I have this feeling," I started, and pointed at her arm, but she flashed her hand in my direction and I stopped. "I know. I have this feeling about a bunch of fucking things," she said. "But we'll take this day first. This day, this breakfast. Then we'll see."

Five months into the new millennium I had reason to go looking for Alejandro. It was said to be the warmest spring in decades and I'd moved into an apartment that for the first time was mine alone, a one-bedroom in Gubbängen with an east-facing balcony where I could read the morning newspaper in the sun. It was only April when the hagberry blossomed, the caul that breaks every year, and an ardent scent suffused the city's green spaces like a stubborn ache, a quiet organic fullness that was new and yet familiar, a slower place in time, with a different center. Sally had gone to India in February with her new love and wrote me long meandering letters whenever she came to a place that had an internet café. I didn't work more than three or four days a week and spent the rest of my time walking around the city. Sitting on a bench in Vasaparken, I remembered the rat Niki and I had found there one summer morning, dense with maggots and death, exposed to the sharp morning light. On a Saturday in early May I knocked on the door of the apartment in Örnsberg, but the woman who opened didn't know an Alejandro. She'd lived abroad for a year and rented the apartment to someone who had evidently sublet it in turn, and when she came home, it had been clean and tidy aside from a shirt and a couple of hair ties in the bathroom. "You're saying you lived here with him? With this Alejandro guy?" Behind her in the hall was the familiar wallpaper, pale blue with French lilies in a darker blue, the wooden floor and the rag rug and the white-painted doorframe to the living room. "No, but I spent some time here. We spent some time here. I figured he might have left an address. Or a phone number." She shook her head. A child called for her from inside the apartment and I said thanks and turned around. "Hold on," she said and went inside. She came back with a little bag holding a dirty white shirt and three red elastics, each equipped with a number of black hairs. "I was going to throw it out anyway," she said. Later that day I made my way to the band's rehearsal space on Gävlegatan, where I encountered Jens behind the bass. His fingers swept along the neck of the instrument in a monotonous bass line. There was a mattress with a sleeping bag in a corner and a pot with dried leftover noodles on the counter. He followed my gaze. "Well, this is me. Coffee?" I nodded. Jens put away his instrument, flicked on the machine, and got out a tin of ground coffee. Alejandro had gone abroad and nobody had seen him for months, he told me, even though they had multiple shows booked for the spring. "Of course the rest of us played anyway, obviously, but it wasn't the same." He set two cups on the table and looked at me with his palms to the sky. "To be honest it was a disaster. People left in the intermission. The promoter canceled the rest of the tour." Jens didn't know where Alejandro was and had no address or phone number to him, "Not even a real name." He didn't expect Alejandro to ever show up again. "That's just how it is with some people, right?" he said. "They blow through your life." He was facing the little sink with his back toward me. "Real name?" I said. "What do you mean by *real name*?" Jens turned to me. "You know, I kind of had the sense that Alejandro was an artist name of some sort. That his real name was different." The coffee was done and he moved the pot to the table while I unbuttoned my coat and sat down. "Okay," he said when he saw my belly, "okay, I can see why you want to get hold of him." The coffee was disgusting, but I drank some anyway while we talked, Jens was going on tour with another band the following week and added my number to his phone in case he'd hear from Alejandro against all odds. "Well, good luck then," he said as I was leaving. He made a sweeping gesture, "You know, with everything."

Jens called me about a year or so ago and suddenly I was compelled to dig out Zomby Woof's CD, and there were a couple of seconds when I stood in the living room, confused with the shiny disc in my hand and no machine to put it in. The cover's black-and-white photo of Alejandro was blurry and grainy and some of the words' letters disappeared in the black of his hair. They had made no effort on the design or even the production, which I recalled as amateurish, with long and inaccessible solos. There wasn't even a hint of a "hit" on it and I don't think anyone ever bothered to send it to any radio stations. Zomby Woof was a live orchestra, their music wasn't of the sort you sing along with on the radio, and the CD was a byproduct, a bonus available for a short time at cost in the bar or at the register when the band was playing. But times had changed, Jens informed me. He was calling with an urgent matter, "a really fucking important question." I felt we could deal with this matter over the phone, but he wanted to come over, and it was urgent, he said, "because the world has finally caught up to Zomby Woof." I pictured him behind the double bass on the side of the drum set, a chapel master of sorts with round spectacles and musical fervor, a head shorter than his instrument. He came over later that afternoon and told me that a radio station in Berlin had started to play their songs, "around the clock, nonstop," and that it had spread to several other German radio stations. He could only guess as to how an example of this long-forgotten CD had ended up in Berlin, but now the interest was "huge" and he was considering a tour. Here was Jens, at my kitchen table, fiddling with the cup of tea I had put in front of him. He was wearing square glasses and his hair was gray and cut in a short, modern style, and he only vaguely resembled the enthusiastic bass player with the long fingers. My two teen children filtered through the kitchen and he didn't pay them any notice. In between us, on the table, the reason for all the commotion, the CD I no longer had the equipment to play. It was out of the question to print more records. "We need to get on Spotify," he said. I scrutinized his face, but he wasn't joking. "Then we'll follow up with club shows in Berlin and elsewhere, maybe a few larger concerts." They were gaining a following in the Netherlands and Belgium, too, he said, "maybe in Japan." Jens was substituting as a music teacher and neither he nor any of the other members in the band had any intention of rejecting this opportunity.

"You know, young people are so nerdy these days, they really get it." He asked if I'd seen any of the clips circulating online. "From the shows. Old video recordings that people are uploading now that we're starting to get big again." There were a couple of words in that sentence that I'd have liked to put a pair of scratching fingers around, like "big" and "again" but I just said that I would look up the clips as soon as I had the chance. "And you don't know where he is?" A piercing feeling in my stomach, around the solar plexus. I shook my head. "No idea." Jens surveyed the kitchen, scanning the walls and shelves as if they might provide a clue. "Do you even know if he's alive?" I shrugged. "I can't say I do. But I feel like I would sense it, somewhere in my body. If he died, I mean." I put a hand at the center of my chest to show. And then I saw in Jens's face that it wasn't Alejandro he was asking about, not at all—that is to say, he wasn't asking for my old Alejandro, but rather the holder of the copyright to the music he hoped would finally generate some income. They owned the rights together. "I feel like it might get complicated if he's gone," Jens said, "you know, technically speaking, financially speaking." He slipped his arms into his jacket again and we bent over his phone while he pulled up one of the concert clips that someone had uploaded to YouTube, but he couldn't get it to work. I promised to get in touch if I ever heard from Alejandro. "Follow me on the 'gram," Jens said before turning to leave. "Everything is on there." Right then there was the catching sound of a key inserted into the lock, followed by my eldest daughter entering the hall. She and Jens looked at each other without a word, and then he turned to me with his eyebrows raised. I nodded. Those black curls, those eyes, that mouth, the whole soft face: unmistakable. Later that evening I looked up Jens's Instagram account, which was dominated by Zomby Woof's presumed comeback, or "super comeback" as he put it in his captions. I clicked on one of the links, but my phone was too old and refused some kind of format. "And maybe Japan"; I thought about how Alejandro would have snickered at that phrase.

4

Birgitte

We live so many lives within our lives—smaller lives with people who come and go, friends who disappear, children who grow up—and I never know which of these lives is meant to serve as the frame. But whenever I'm in the grips of a fever or infatuation there is no confusion; my "self" recedes and gives space to a nameless joy, a unified whole that preserves all the details, inseparable and distinct, next to one another. Afterward I always remember this state as one of grace. That might be one way of describing the whole, people filing in and out of my face in no particular order. No "beginning" and no "end," no chronology, only each and every moment and what transpires therein. At this point, now that I've started writing, there's one person I can't escape. Birgitte. I used to think that a sharper sense of being alive was to be found in the forest, that I would be able to walk my way to it between the tall pines, that I would find it while sitting alone on a tree stump with the sun in my eyes, or while gazing out on the sea from some rocks on the shore; that I could only be fully awake among the silent elements. But it turned out that I already had everything right here, in the details around me, that it's simply a question of being attentive in looking at all of it, of letting myself go and directing my attention outward, and I mean truly *outward*. That's where this sharper sense of being alive is found, in the alert gaze on another. It was how I came to understand Birgitte, by observing her attentively.

An incident in her early teens scarred her mentally and she developed a withdrawn personality colored by churning anxiety. Within the span of an hour she died and was reborn as a different person; there was a flip in her mind that moved the unfathomable event to the far back where it was quarantined from the rest of the world, out of reach for the rest of her life, securely wrapped and stowed away. I don't think Birgitte ever went there during her waking hours. The only time she talked about the incident was thirty years after the fact, and only with one other person, and it is my guess that she in so doing discovered that the incident was no longer an "incident" she still remembered, but more like a color or a fractal, not even a memory as such but rather the place from which all memories came, a shadow that respired in the background of her life every day. I assume this is how a singular experience affects a person; the event gets encapsulated with the poison still intact, seeping, a slow command. It's well-known that whoever coined the expression "what doesn't kill you makes you stronger" has never met a rape victim.

Granted, she'd been fragile even before this happened; the vulnerability-stress model we use today to explain how traumatic experiences have such a different impact on different people would've helped me understand her better. It might even have helped her understand herself better. She was a timid child. No older than seven when her father died, which happened suddenly the day after his appendicitis surgery; the living room was soiled by blood and stomach contents when the ambulance drove off. With the funeral over the father was not to be mentioned again; the family (she had two siblings) entered a new phase. I imagine it as a grayish trance state, a dull, diligent life, where their mother, who'd originally been a homemaker, took on two paid jobs (as a housekeeper at the town hotel and as a caretaker at the nursing home) to keep the family afloat. The children grew practiced at their responsibilities and as teenagers they started to work on weekends and school holidays to help provide for the family. There wasn't time for much more than work and sleep. Words like *psychology*, *trauma*, and *processing* weren't part of most people's vocabulary, and when she crawled into her older sister's bed at the wolf hour while pretending to mumble "father, father" in her sleep, the sister covered Birgitte's mouth with her hand until she stopped and opened her eyes. The family visited the grave on the days prescribed by the calendar, when the mother would roll a thin, embroidered handkerchief around her finger, using it to catch her tears before they left the corner of her eye. There wasn't much to say in these moments. Much later, when Birgitte and I walked around the cemetery a few miles south of Stavanger, looking for her parents' grave (I had to make her take me there), she reluctantly told me about her father, his big hands, his good intentions, the pedantic order of the tool shop he ran. We brushed off a dusting of snow and laid down our flowers at the stone inscribed with their names and dates. Then she looked at me and shook her head; even now there was nothing to say. So Birgitte was already a silenced teenager by the time she was babysitting for one of her mother's acquaintances and the man of the house came home earlier than agreed upon and the child had just fallen asleep in the cot. The pay, twenty kronor for four hours of work, was already in Birgitte's skirt pocket. She was open, vulnerable, anticipating new catastrophes, already worried about new catastrophes, already aware of what another catastrophe might do to her. I imagine she saw the incident happen even before she met his gaze as he stood with his back to the door. Many years later I started working at an inpatient psychiatric clinic in Stockholm, and at this job I met people who reminded me of Birgitte. The things they had been subjected to lingered in me long past the end of my shifts, and their anxiety was like hers, an anxiety that doesn't wax

and wane but endures in the form of a tension inside everything. Theirs is not laughter but anxious laughter, anxious
joy, anxious walking, an anxious way of talking. I was inti-
mately familiar with Birgitte's anxiety since it showed up
when she did and lingered in every room she entered. Like
everything, this changed with the passing of time, but it
also did not. Though she was the youngest, she was the first
of the siblings to move away from home, to become her own.
Well, *almost* her own, since it didn't take her long to realize
that being "one's own" was a privilege reserved for those
who were more fortunate, such that she could be "her own"
only if she leaned against someone or something. A man.
A group. A clearly defined system. She was politically active
in the sixties and seventies, joined new movements, got an
education, tried drugs, hitchhiked through Europe, played
the guitar and sang in a folk rock band, wore soft purples
with her dark hair billowing down to her waist, but I can't
quite view her political engagement as authentic, perhaps
because I've never heard her provide an analysis any deeper
than "it was a really dumb war" (about Vietnam), "why
should they get to decide everything?" (about US imperial-
ism), and "cars smell bad" (the environment). She drifted
whichever way the wind blew—not because she was placid
or obsequious, but because it was all she could do. An inescapable drive to adapt, that's what he left her with, the
man whose child she'd been watching and who sent her out
the door as he fumbled with his belt afterward. A minute

later he opened the door again and tossed out her coat. To adapt and blend in, to blend in so much that she disappeared: it was either that or losing her mind. I had the sense that madness and brokenness had been the only option for many of the patients I met at the inpatient ward in Stockholm decades later. Birgitte had been able to adapt, and she adapted to such a degree that what defined her personality was an absence of personality. Collectivities suited her well for this reason, and she enjoyed the early seventies. "Like a fish in water," was how she described herself. *Like a fish in a school of fish*, I thought to myself. The eighties, with their dogma of success and competition, wasn't as good of a match for her. She was in no way an "individual" of the sort stipulated by the eighties and every decade thereafter in the western world. Her avoidant character became obvious to see, and I think people viewed her as uninteresting and bland. And she probably was uninteresting; I imagine it was hard for people around her to remember whether she'd been present for an event or a meeting. "Was Birgitte at the party last Friday?" Impossible to recall, if someone would even think to ask. "Did Birgitte say anything at the meeting yesterday?" Hard to tell, hard to remember. "Was she even there?" Nobody could say one way or another. When community disappeared and people retreated into their own private lives, Birgitte sort of stayed behind, incapable of taking an initiative or a stand on her own. Her efforts to blend in and avoid friction obliterated the part of her where an individual character should have formed with all its desires and roughness, a spine with its own bristles. Instead there was only anxiety, vibrating and surface-level, exacting and constant, the only aspect of Birgitte that was visible to others.

Most people who are worried about going mad don't go mad, but when Birgitte was twenty-three years old, she had a psychotic break. It happened in the late sixties, in early November, on the Sunday she gave birth to me. A couple of hours into labor at Malmö's General Hospital my heart stopped, and Birgitte saw true concern in the nurse's gaze, real worry, which she could only interpret as a sign that another catastrophe was coming. It had been too long; I must have gotten stuck in there. My dad was sitting on a stool in the corridor, doing the crossword. I picture him wearing clogs and jeans and a corduroy blazer with a National Liberation Front pin on the collar, sideburns and hair down to his neck, and when the staff ran past him, he tried to understand what was happening. A mere three years later, when my sister was born at Söder's Hospital in Stockholm, it wasn't even a question that he would be present in the delivery room. I was born by vacuum extraction, but by the time I finally landed on Birgitte's stomach, screaming and bright red, already curious about her, already pissed at her, she was far away, gone inside herself. She was quiet and sleepless in the maternity ward, roosting on a madness that exploded when we got home to the apartment at Slottsgatan where her anxiety grew, became manic, feverish. She took walks with the stroller and yelled at people she felt were staring at her, or she closed the curtains in the bedroom and cried in the dark for hours on end, only to get up afterward as if nothing had happened. My dad and I got skilled at bottle feeding, long walks, and luring her to a doctor he knew and who gave her sleeping pills. Food and sleep, said the doctor, whose son had done military service with my dad. Food and sleep, it's the only thing that helps, and routines, walks, and sympathy from family and friends. In fact, he told us, there was just one thing we should avoid: the care that was on offer at the time, i.e., the "mental hospitals" that admitted people in the state Birgitte was in, since they rarely discharged anyone who had been admitted. At the close of one of these visits, the doctor gestured for my dad to come. I was sleeping in the stroller which was parked by the door; Birgitte leaned over me, adjusting something. "She shouldn't be left alone with the child, of course," the doctor said. I can picture the way the two men looked at her, her unruly mass of hair, her shawl in the same bright red as the dress, her tall winter boots, her dirty cuticles and the palpably quivering expressions behind the makeup. These little signs of madness, unmistakable, as if she'd been dropped into a new country and been made to put on the national dress, and whenever I look at pictures from that time (my dad is a photographer and never put the camera down), I am usually able to date it based on her gaze, her nails, the way her elaborate outfits fall from her body. "Ah, *that* period." The first winter, before we moved and things got better. My dad spent hours lying next to me, moving his finger back and forth over the bridge of my nose to help me come to rest. My cot was placed outside the bathroom, which he used as a darkroom at night, developing and copying photographs. He worked as an assistant to a famous photographer, who was also the person who got us the apartment. Birgitte slept through the nights and the mornings, and when she woke up, we made excursions tailored to the state she was in, most of the time walks and café visits. When she started to get better, we were able to call on people we knew, and in due time she was able to let others pick me up and hold me, even leave the room with me. With my dad's arm around her shoulders she learned to deal with her anxiety. Maybe "deal with" is not the right phrase; "bear" might be a better way to put it, or "survive," since her body remained tense and she continued to scan the environment for disasters in the making, a glass too close to an edge, an unsheathed knife on the table, a burning cigarette in an ashtray, a hole in the hedge of someone's garden. This world remained a dangerous place for the rest of her life, dangerous to all, an unbearable place, in no way made for people. There was too much uncertainty, with the future and everything that can go awry, everything that might fall and break or start a fire, all the accidents just waiting to happen, the burglaries, the collisions, the floods, the fevers, the apocalypse. Anxiety's central task, as instructed by fear, is to run ahead and touch everything, circle potentialities with the intention of preventing them from happening, on and on and on in a process that never stops, that becomes one with life. As a child I would sometimes watch Birgitte when we'd borrowed a motorboat to go to the archipelago. She would sit on a flat rock with her face in the sun, and I'd notice that she didn't close her eyes for more than a few seconds at a time before she looked up, squinting, quickly checking the surroundings, apparently involuntarily, as if compelled by something inside of her. She was never granted peace, there was always some aspect of the world that had to be controlled lest things went out of hand. And I suppose that's what's at the heart of it for every person suffering from anxiety; the fact that life, by its very nature, is impossible to manage.

That first winter she only dipped into the netherworld and turned right back up again. Life remained the playing field for her inner struggles, but the screaming and the madness vanished along with the darting gaze, the dirty fingers that could never relax, the paranoia right under her skin which always kept her on her toes. We moved to Stockholm (where my dad got a job at a magazine), and a new, much more comfortable period took over, with childcare, a career (Birgitte was a Swedish literature teacher), demonstrations, parties, picnics with brännboll games in the Haga Park. I know exactly how to date the pictures from this time, me sitting in the stroller in the middle of Hamngatan holding a sign—*peace!*—and Birgitte pushing the stroller, wearing no makeup and in relaxed pants and a backpack, at ease in the likeminded crowd, smiling at the camera. "Oh, *that* period." We were living in Solna, then on Kocksgatan, then at my dad's mother's in Jakobsberg, then in a house in Salem, then on Hälsingegatan, then across from Kronobergs-parken, and finally in Farsta where they at last found an opening for my sister and me at a daycare center. We went to parties where the discussions were lively, my dad disliked Soviet- and Chinese-style communism and eagerly shared this opinion with everyone he met, even the communists, perhaps the communists especially, and he was forever at the center of debates that grew more intense as the night wore on. He was never silent, could not be silent, especially not when it came to communism. He argued that an ideology that can't be put into practice without killing its opponents deserves nothing but scorn, and he was horrified that so many held this ideology for the best *despite* the exorbitant number of people who'd been imprisoned and murdered and starved in its name. He was very clear on that point, and the later the hour, the more keen he was to expound on his views. His favorite position was opposing the popular argument that communism was a good idea *in theory* and for this reason had real value ("This bridge looks good but unfortunately it collapses as soon as someone tries to drive across."). When I think about my parents during this era, that's the image that comes to mind: my father with his dirty corn pipe on the couch, debating more people than most would bother with, confident and alone, so intensely alive and political, and then there's Birgitte in the background, it takes a second before I even see her, she blends so well with the background, Birgitte who would never raise her voice to express a view of her own, or oppose anyone, or have the courage to be a rebel among rebels like my father. When she spoke, it was usually to agree with the previous speaker, and she was wholly ready to change her mind were someone else to appear more convincing, careful to express herself with enough vagueness and uncertainty that what she said allowed for every possible interpretation. She avoided offense and conflict at every cost, which meant that she disliked the way my father was a constant magnet for irritation. At the start of the party, when people were smoking and eating in the kitchen, when my sister and I were playing in one of the rooms, when there was one or many bottles of wine on the table, my dad's opinions served as a piquant feature of the party. He was known to be intelligent and sociable, he had lots of stories and was a good photographer. As the night wore on, when the cigarette smoke thickened and us kids were stretched out on the floor or in one of the beds reading comics, when people switched to Campari and gin and empty bottles crowded the floor of the pantry, the tone would grow more heated. Was he a member of the bourgeoisie, that photographer with the sideburns? At this point it wasn't long before my sister and I would be asleep in some bed or other, snug next to each other and well aware that Birgitte had secretly kept an eye on us through the night, it wasn't long before some would start dancing, hands aloft, next to the bookcase with the gramophone, by which time my dad would be parked on the kitchen sofa, sticking to his beliefs in a hailstorm of disagreements from his ideological opponents. When he tells me about this period today, he says there was no limit to the silly things people said and believed. He's eighty-three years old and still politically left wing ("whatever that means nowadays"), nuanced and specific, and believes that the main change, the lasting success of this period, was not had in the issues as such, not in party politics, maybe not even in the struggle, but rather in interpersonal relations, the way people started talking to each other; the fact that he, the son of a single mother who worked as a house cleaner, could be debating the sons of architects and daughters of teachers, that they could curse one another out and that he didn't have to apologize, that they shared space on equal terms. My dad frequently reminds me that my grandmother would put on her best clothes for a doctor's appointment, that she would take the stairs when she saw a higher-status neighbor waiting for the elevator, and he is careful to point out how utterly foreign it would be for me or him to behave like that. "There's the legacy of that time," he says, "the true revolution." Most of his old friends have dementia or are dead, but he keeps the conversation going, with himself or his wife who is only sixty years old, he subscribes to *Time* and the *Economist*, listens to radio documentaries, reads books. He lives in a house with a small garden in Rönninge and says that every day is a good day. We never talk about Birgitte anymore, but he was the person she finally opened up to, and a few weeks after her funeral he told me about her, told me everything he knew about her, her catastrophes, gave me all she'd entrusted to him. They'd been divorced for fifteen years and he nevertheless cried for her life, a life lived but also spilled.

Articles about anxiety often note that it was historically useful, so evolution made it part of our nature. Anxiety motivated us to make sure the fire was out and the children still breathing; it protected us in teaching us to protect ourselves and others. It's a simple sorting mechanism: the Stone Age people who anxiously scanned the forest for predators survived, while anyone who wandered carelessly in between the trees was eaten. We, today's living, are the descendants of our anxious ancestors. When I visit Birgitte's grave at Skogskyrkogården, I wonder what her life would have been without anxiety, but it's no easier to picture than imagining a day without weather. It was one with her, this survival mechanism that became her lifelong shield and disability, a minor function run amok. In some obscure way I can sense it more clearly when I'm at her lonely grave; her fussy care, her little sighs, the way she constantly hummed an inaudible melody that seemed to follow the temperature of her mind. When my friends came over, I would pretend like she wasn't there. It was easier that way. It's what most of my classmates did, since most of them also had parents who were odd one way or another, moms who were out drunk on the couch in the afternoon and who yelled at visitors, moms who exploded in different ways, who were at a breaking point beneath the burden of wage work and difficult kids, who cried at PTA meetings or else just seemed old-fashioned and smelled weird, or dads who pulled children's hair or had other families in secret or who got sick and died in the span of a fall semester. It was considered normal, per the established limits of the times; "normal," as my dad would put it with a funny emphasis to indicate how he disdained that term. It must have been that first winter in Malmö, during which Birgitte was all but "normal," that forced him to have a broader perspective. He was open-minded for his time, my dad; he shrugged and leaned in, gave me his ear. Only rarely did he pass judgment, and he never denounced anything. As teenagers, my sister and I rebelled only against him, since he was the one who was present and available, pipe in mouth, to discuss it all, equally willing to accept (bisexuality, alcohol) and wage battles (hashish, school absences). Birgitte was elsewhere, somewhere inside herself, and there was nobody in our family who could bear to direct any anger at those timid eyes. She was in the bedroom, working on something, and left the conflicts for my dad, or else she was reading in bed. I remember seeing *Your Erroneous Zones* in beige softcover on the nightstand, which was later added to a new section of the bookcase that was hers alone. Göran Tunström was the pinnacle of my dad's canon, along with Gunnar Ekelöf, who he made me read as soon as I knew how to sound out two letters combined. The others: Graham Greene, Hemingway, Steinbeck, Eyvind Johnson, Selma Lagerlöf, photo books, and Ed McBain in double rows, along with most of the titles published by Sven Lindqvist, who he adored. He read his *Diary of a Lover* and gave it to me the minute he was done, which awakened me to a new type of language. I was in my early teens and the day before we'd fought until the neighbor banged on the wall; I was furious with the world in general. At breakfast the next morning there was a book waiting for me at my spot, in what turned out to be a long-term loan since I still have it in my bookcase. Every morning was a new beginning for my dad who never let a mood stay overnight. The messy and semi-organized bookcase was shared between them until one day when Birgitte made some space and created a new type of section, in which *Your Erroneous Zones* was the first addition in between yin-yang bookends that she had bought at a store called Aquarius on Drottning-gatan. A new era dawned in that shelf and in her, character-ized by Jung, Janov, Fromm, astrology, magnets, crystals, and tarot cards, and where no theory disqualified another. She had her dreams interpreted and got Ayurvedic massage, piled raw, grated root vegetables on her plate while the rest of us ate dinner, and spent a fortune on a man who suspended an orb attached to a string over her body while directing questions at her organs. Apparently the organs were able to describe their own imbalances through the pendulum. She spent a weekend on Öland smeared in mud and avocado. She went to Jutland and danced African and liberating dances, she took a color workshop after which she dressed exclusively in yellow for a few weeks, she had her aura evaluated by a visiting guru, she made drinks from Chinese powders that smelled like hay, met with mediums, and started drawing little circles over my forehead with her finger before I went to school in the mornings. It never occurred to me to ask her to stop. I was born in the sign of Scorpio, which meant, according to Birgitte, that I had a tendency to be critical and dour, and I didn't wish to willingly confirm this prophecy. Statements like "Your chakras are imbalanced" or "Mondays are good for strong yin" passed with no comment from the rest of the family. She stopped reading the news since it sabotaged the valuable energies of the morning hours. At a séance in the basement of some acquaintance she let imported snails crawl over her back for hours, a treatment intended to cleanse the body from unspecified toxins. She fasted for weeks on end, did yogic enemas, rinsed her nose with saltwater, and rubbed my hands with coconut oil when my skin was dry. "Every item they sell at the pharmacy has toxins in it." It's easy to date the photos from this era. We're in the archipelago, a rented cabin on Ingarö, it's early fall, Birgitte's hair is frizzy and henna dyed, she's wearing a suede jacket with shoulder pads and a yin-yang necklace. Always this yin-yang symbol, though I've never heard a satisfying explanation of its significance. Almost ten years later I would travel by train through the Soviet Union and Mongolia to get to Peking, and during my eight months in Southeast Asia I never saw the yin-yang symbol used in any other context than as merchandise for tourists like Birgitte. The photo shows her looking anemic after weeks of fasting on fruit. The summer has come to an end and we're about to leave the cabin on Ingarö. "Ah, *that* period." My sister is in a lounge chair at the center of the photo, cradling a guitar, and my dad stands next to her, holding the remote shutter to the camera he must have placed on the windowsill, and Birgitte's gaze is distant, almost evasive. She might already be fretting about the drive home, about not leaving anything behind, about not crashing, about everyone wearing their seatbelt, about finding a parking spot and not getting a ticket. I'm in the background, on my way out of the frame, in black cloth slippers and a thick, tattered softcover in my hand, *Winter in Paradise.* Anyone who writes about nature the way Ulf Lundell does has no other duty to this world. Birgitte probably called herself a "seeker" during this period, and maybe she'd have claimed to have found something. I suppose most people who seek in earnest do end up finding something sooner or later, if the seeking is true, if it's founded in a sincere desire to know oneself, to look seriously behind that familiar face in the mirror. I have met many "seekers," who may or may not have used that term for themselves, and I suppose I am one myself, but when it comes to Birgitte I doubt that the seeking was more than an evasive gesture, a pose, a new way of being superficial. When I use that word, "superficial," I don't mean "banal," but rather "incapable," robbed of the ability to be authentic. Like anyone with intense anxiety, she was perpetually floating toward the surface, consumed with keeping the world in place and looking out for potential dangers. Her anxiety kept her living at surface level, and it might be fair to say that she was banal in that sense, helplessly, against her own will. Going deeper requires a loss of control, requires the abandonment of that constant surveillance of time and space in exchange for a headlong fall inside oneself, or into somebody else, or down one of life's many cracks and fissures. I believe that she spoke about these things with a priest she went to for a time; Lars-Åke, "a true healer, let me tell you." Birgitte saw no contradiction between her many sprawling belief systems; God, Jesus, and the Zodiac; auras and crystals; psychics and stones and healing mud. It all blended together and that which worked, worked; this was how Birgitte saw it. What Lars-Åke thought of it all, I couldn't say, but when we met before her funeral (which he officiated, at her request) he looked at me with the face of someone who knows though he cannot speak. And he put such a kind hand on my shoulder after my eulogy. Other than by looks, he said, and I nodded, already knowing what he was about to say, you don't resemble her at all.

And the end? Better than expected and still terrible, mangled by illness over the course of a few months when she took so many benzodiazepines for her anxiety that her eyes were hazy from lunch onward, with pupils that floated around and got stuck staring at the pattern on the wall by her bed for hours. Her partner (Petter, the last man she had) held her hand and talked to her without getting a response, which didn't seem to bother him. In the final weeks language was the first to go, then sight, and she basically just lay there mumbling, but she moved her hands enthusiastically as soon as she heard my voice. Maybe she had something she wanted to say. I sat by her bed and thought about world literature and film history, the multitude of scenes like this one, when someone, in their final moments, is at last able to reach out and say something important, scenes of explanation, a "forgive me" or some soothing words, and how the position I was in was so rarely portrayed, this sense that it was too late, that something had been in vain, that not even this last void between us could be explained or put into words. Nothing was done, no "forgive me" was said, to the extent that there was even a reason to say it, and which one of us would have said it I still don't know. Her breathing was so anxious through the end, her anxiety the last to leave the body. But shortly thereafter, when her partner had gone to tell the nurses it was over, I felt her streak past, right by me. Finally you're free of all this, I thought.

She had started on the benzodiazepines already in the late eighties, shortly after the divorce, when my sister forced her to go see a doctor for help with her sleeping troubles. Perhaps there was an answer of sorts to Birgitte's search after all, somewhere in that dampening chemistry. The round white pills came in boxes of a hundred each, and later when I helped organize her things and was emptying her bathroom cabinets I understood that she'd had several doctors prescribing them to her, and that she'd even traveled to Norway to get more. I pictured her at the clinics, her fragile charm and the timid eyes and the names of the drugs she mentioned as if in passing, with the pleading voice that men around her always seemed to respond to. She was clear on her primary need, which was to secure *lasting protection*, and most of the men she met were happy to provide it in accordance with their ability. After the divorce was finalized they lined up for her affection, the men who wished to protect and love, they were men she knew who were single or newly separated and some of them still married, and they were new acquaintances she met at the bars and restaurants and dinners that her girlfriends dragged her to. Birgitte wasn't particularly adorable anymore, but everything that appealed to these men's instincts to help, shore up, guide, and understand, was still there. I no longer lived at home and didn't see her a lot during this period, but my sister was there and she told me about the men she bumped into in the kitchen eating filmjölk in the mornings, the men she encountered when they rang the doorbell late at night with flowers in hand. Birgitte was able to pick and choose, though that's probably not how she experienced it, and some men stayed for a month while others had to slouch off as the night wore on, the flowers they'd brought left in a vase on the kitchen table. In hindsight it might look like she had the upper hand, suitors competing for her favor, but of course their protection had terms. There were clauses to their goodwill. Her anxiety could seem so crazy, so deranged and psychiatric and primitive, but outside our family, meaning the family made up by her, my sister, me, and our dad, she was able to tame it into the range of what's considered normal. This lifelong undertaking, the effort to make her instability seem normal, was her life's great struggle, the great stipulation for being touched by the love of others. Once she'd started on the pills it was easier and she didn't want to stop, *couldn't* stop, and Petter, who she met at a dinner party a year after the divorce, did not see her iris, not on that night nor any of the nights that followed, but he came to adore her nevertheless. She smiles so big at the camera in the pictures from their travels together, mostly to Gran Canaria. They probably had a compact camera with autofocus, a silver-colored model with zoom and flash built in, and they must have asked a passerby to take their picture. They're at a restaurant table or standing on a beach or a cliff with the sea in the background, photos that are so similar they invite confusion with the hundreds of other photographs I have seen from places like this, as if they were all taken from a communal fantasy about vacations in the sun. She looks more filled out, her hair is dyed and arranged in a bun, and Petter is usually positioned at an angle behind her as if prepared for episodes of collapse and sudden loss of control. He was the most stable of all the men she met, financially independent and not interested in any drama, with adult children and cropped curls following an intact hairline. They thought about marriage, but then she got sick for the first time. Monumental angst, the little white friends disappeared from their boxes at unprecedented speed, and when I went to visit I found her sitting on the couch, straight as a rod, sobbing in panic. It was half a year before the turn of the millennium, she wasn't even fifty-five years old. Petter was stroking her back, and it didn't seem like she noticed. "We're going to get through this," he said, and I was grateful that he wanted to be a "we" with Birgitte. I never saw her express any great passion for Petter, but she did get a few years of tranquility until the second and final bout of the illness; under his protection and behind the scrim of her white friends she was once more a survivor of sorts, despite it all.

When I gave birth to my daughter (Söder's Hospital, nineteen hours, Sally cut the umbilical cord), Birgitte and Petter came to see us the next day, and the child instantly fell asleep in Birgitte's arms. Petter and I were chatting, they'd been on a trip down Spain's Atlantic coastline, but she didn't speak, she just sat there, absolutely still as she looked at the sleeping girl. Her first daughter's first child in her arms; something soothing about it perhaps, a respite. Maybe it pushed doomsday a little further into the future, as if she had finally attached to something, touched ground and put a stake in time. She and my daughter got a couple of years together, but for my twin sons Birgitte is just a gravestone and a black-and-white photograph in the corner of my bedroom mirror. In November we usually buy cressets and go to Skogskyrkogården, where we meet Sally and her kids at the entrance (her dad's grave is a quarter mile from Birgitte's) and as we walk between the stones the years pass sideways around us behind their flimsy curtains. As far as the dead are concerned, chronology has no import and all that matters are the details, the degree of density, this *how* and *what* and everything to do with *who*. When I was younger I often thought I should travel more and farther, spend more time in foreign countries, that I should be in a constant state of velocity so that I could get out there and truly live, but with time I have come to understand that everything I was looking for was right here, inside of me, inside the things that surround me, in the money jobs that became my actual jobs, in the constancy of the everyday, in the eyes of the people I meet when I allow my gaze to linger. I'm writing again after the fever, as if an old, welcome wound has opened and started to bleed, and I guess it's an incomplete puzzle, these pictures of others and whoever they end up portraying. At one grave or another Sally will get out a thermos and toast to the headstones around us. "Soon it will be too late," she says, and hands me the thermos. "And that's why we have to exert ourselves to the utmost."

A Note from the Translator

As the temperatures start to drop in September and the long Scandinavian summer days shorten, the Swedish book industry and its readers flock to the Gothenburg Book Fair. It's the biggest literary event of the year; for the duration of one long weekend, the city's cavernous exhibition hall is abuzz with author talks, debates, gossip, and book slinging. In 2022 I attended as part of a group of translators invited by the Swedish Arts Council. Introductions revealed that no fewer than four of us were working on Ia Genberg's *Detaljerna*. There we were, a little contingent in love with the labor of bringing every wrinkle of Genberg's finely drawn portraits into Dutch, Simplified Chinese, German, and English.

Four already seemed like a lot, but in actual fact we were merely a fraction of the horde of translators contracted by twenty-seven publishing houses around the world to translate this book. *Detaljerna*, published earlier that year, had been a runaway success and would go on to win the prestigious August Prize in November. It's the fourth novel from Ia Genberg, who debuted at forty-five after leaving a career in journalism and retraining as a nurse in order to be able to save her writing for fiction.

In some ways *Detaljerna* was an unexpected sensation. It's a quiet book, comprised of four chronicles of mostly ordinary people, a novel where "nothing really happens." That quiet, however, holds a grace that vaults the sum total of quotidian moments into something more expansive. It's not the only novel to come out of Scandinavia with a bloodhound's nose for pursuing a scent, but Genberg is no Karl Ove Knausgaard. Genberg's narrator emerges refractively through her relationships as opposed to via forensic excavation of childhood memories; everything in this book is leaning on something else. Walking through a cemetery with her best friend, the narrator watches as "the years pass sideways around us behind their flimsy curtains. As far as the dead are concerned, chronology has no import and all that matters are the details, the degree of density, this *how* and *what* and everything to do with *who*."

Genberg's concern with that density was reflected in her writing process for the book. She started over from the beginning of whichever chapter she was working on each time she sat down to write, rethreading the entire cloth of the text countless of times. The result is long, winding sentences with multiple clauses that are somehow never difficult or tedious to read. (An interesting challenge for the

English translation, a language in which a "run-on sentence" is a bad thing. Reader, some of these phrases were longer yet in the Swedish.)

At the bookfair, a portion of the Genberg contingent decided to seek out the author in the crush. She was a popular guest with the many media and civil society organizations that put on discussions and interviews for the general audience, and we caught her mid interview with a priest from the Swedish Church. Genberg, dressed in gray faded jeans, a gray-striped shirt with an open collar, and a black blazer paired with bright-red sneakers, was just stepping off the stage when I introduced our vague mission by blurting out "Hi, we're your translators!" Ia was needed at the book signing table and surely had to rush off to her next event, but instead of brushing us off, she gave us an amused, somewhat astonished smile. "Wait, but can't we chat for a bit?" she asked, a question that seemed to get to the heart of her writing itself.

Per *The Details*, that openness to the now is all there is. Look closely and every moment becomes dense with meaning, unfolding backward and forward in time as it makes us who we are. There is no one whole—"the whole is loose at the edges," she noted in one interview—all we have are those fraying threads, flapping in the wind, and the complex ways they tie fast to each other.

Queens, New York
February 2023

Here ends Ia Genberg's
The Details.

The first edition of the book was printed and
bound at Lakeside Book Company
in Harrisonburg, Virginia, August 2023.

A NOTE ON THE TYPE

This novel was set in Century Schoolbook, a transitional serif typeface from the Century typeface family. It was designed in 1919 by Morris Fuller Benton for the American Type Founder at the request of Ginn & Company, a textbook publisher. It became widely popular for its readability and has been used to teach North American children how to read for generations.

HARPERVIA

An imprint dedicated to publishing international voices,
ering readers a chance to encounter other lives and other
oints of view via the language of the imagination.